ECEIVE
AUG 15 2021
BY:

D0962468

Hi, I'm JIMMY!

Like me, you probably noticed the world is run by adults.

But ask yourself: Who would do the best job

of making books that *kids* will love?

Yeah. **Kids!**

So that's how the idea of JIMMY books came to life.

We want every JIMMY book to be so good

that when you're finished, you'll say,

"PLEASE GIVE ME ANOTHER BOOK!"

Give this one a try and see if you agree.

(If not, you're probably an adult!)

JIMMY PATTERSON BOOKS FOR YOUNG READERS

JAMES PATTERSON PRESENTS

Sci-Fi Junior High by John Martin and Scott Seegert
Sci-Fi Junior High: Crash Landing by John Martin and Scott Seegert
How to Be a Supervillain by Michael Fry
How to Be a Supervillain: Born to Be Good by Michael Fry
How to Be a Supervillain: Bad Guys Finish First by Michael Fry
The Unflushables by Ron Bates
Ernestine, Catastrophe Queen by Merrill Wyatt
Scouts by Shannon Greenland

THE MIDDLE SCHOOL SERIES BY JAMES PATTERSON

Middle School, The Worst Years of My Life
Middle School: Get Me Out of Here!
Middle School: Big Fat Liar
Middle School: How I Survived Bullies, Broccoli, and Snake Hill
Middle School: Ultimate Showdown
Middle School: Save Rafe!
Middle School: Just My Rotten Luck
Middle School: Dog's Best Friend
Middle School: Escape to Australia
Middle School: From Hero to Zero
Middle School: Born to Rock
Middle School: Master of Disaster

THE DOG DIARIES SERIES BY JAMES PATTERSON

Dog Diaries
Dog Diaries: Happy Howlidays!
Dog Diaries: Mission Impawsible

THE I FUNNY SERIES BY JAMES PATTERSON

I Funny
I Even Funnier
I Totally Funniest
I Funny TV
I Funny: School of Laughs
The Nerdiest, Wimpiest, Dorkiest I Funny Ever

THE TREASURE HUNTERS SERIES BY JAMES PATTERSON

Treasure Hunters
Treasure Hunters: Danger Down the Nile
Treasure Hunters: Secret of the Forbidden City
Treasure Hunters: Peril at the Top of the World
Treasure Hunters: Quest for the City of Gold
Treasure Hunters: All-American Adventure
Treasure Hunters: The Plunder Down Under

THE HOUSE OF ROBOTS SERIES BY JAMES PATTERSON

House of Robots
House of Robots: Robots Go Wild!
House of Robots: Robot Revolution

THE DANIEL X SERIES BY JAMES PATTERSON

The Dangerous Days of Daniel X
Daniel X: Watch the Skies
Daniel X: Demons and Druids
Daniel X: Game Over
Daniel X: Armageddon
Daniel X: Lights Out

OTHER ILLUSTRATED NOVELS AND STORIES

Katt Vs. Dogg
Max Einstein: The Genius Experiment
Max Einstein: Rebels with A Cause
Max Einstein: Saves the Future
Pottymouth and Stoopid
Unbelievably Boring Bart
Not So Normal Norbert
Laugh Out Loud
Jacky Ha-Ha
Jacky Ha-Ha: My Life Is a Joke
Jacky Ha-Ha: The Graphic Novel
Public School Superhero
Word of Mouse
Give Please a Chance
Give Thank You a Try
Big Words for Little Geniuses
Bigger Word for Little Geniuses
Cuddly Critters for Little Geniuses
The Candies Save Christmas

For exclusives, trailers, and other information, visit jimmypatterson.org.

TREASURE HUNTERS

THE PLUNDER DOWN UNDER

BY JAMES PATTERSON

AND CHRIS GRABENSTEIN

ILLUSTRATED BY

JULIANA NEUFELD

JIMMY PATTERSON BOOKS

LITTLE, BROWN AND COMPANY

NEW YORK BOSTON LONDON

JIMMY Patterson Books / Little, Brown and Company
Hachette Book Group
1290 Avenue of the Americas, New York, NY 10104
JamesPatterson.com

First Edition: June 2020

JIMMY Patterson Books is an imprint of Little, Brown and Company, a division of Hachette Book Group, Inc. The Little, Brown name and logo are trademarks of Hachette Book Group, Inc. The JIMMY Patterson Books® name and logo are trademarks of JBP Business, LLC.

The publisher is not responsible for websites (or their content) that are not owned by the publisher.

The Hachette Speakers Bureau provides a wide range of authors for speaking events. To find out more, go to hachettespeakersbureau.com or call (866) 376-6591.

Library of Congress Cataloging-in-Publication Data
Names: Patterson, James, author. | Grabenstein, Chris, author. | Neufeld, Juliana, 1982- illustrator.
Title: The plunder down under / by James Patterson and Chris Grabenstein; illustrated by Juliana Neufeld.
Description: First edition. | New York: JIMMY Patterson Books/Little, Brown, 2020. | Series: treasure hunters; book 7 | Audience: Ages 7-12. | Audience: Grades 2-3. | Summary: Bick, Beck, Storm, and Tommy have one week to traverse the Australian Outback, locate Charlotte Badger and her pirate cronies, and find evidence to prove their parents innocent of stealing rare opals.
Identifiers: LCCN 2020004777 (print) | LCCN 2020004778 (ebook) | ISBN 9780316420587 (board) | ISBN 9780316420600 (ebook)
Subjects: CYAC: Adventure and adventurers—Fiction. | Pirates—Fiction. | False imprisonment—Fiction. | Buried treasure—Fiction. | Brothers and sisters—Fiction. | Twins—Fiction. | Australia—Fiction.
Classification: LCC PZ7.P27653 Plu 2020 (print) | LCC PZ7.P27653 (ebook) | DDC [Fic]—dc23
LC record available at https://lccn.loc.gov/2020004777
LC ebook record available at https://lccn.loc.gov/2020004778

10 9 8 7 6 5 4 3 2 1

LSC-C

Printed in the United States of America

For my niece Rachel
and everybody else working for
the National Park Service.
—CG

ATLANTIC OCEAN

AFRI

THERE ARE
2,0
LANGUA
SPOKEN
WO

PEOPLE LIVED HERE AS LONG AGO AS 9000 B.C. THAT'S A LONG TIME!

SOUTH AMERICA

ANTA

THE WORLD ACCORDING TO THE KIDDS!

ARCTIC OCEAN

THE HIMALAYAS ARE THE TALLEST MOUNTAINS IN THE WORLD! MOUNT EVEREST IS 8,849 METERS /29,035 FT.

PACIFIC OCEAN

INDIAN OCEAN

TONGA

THE SANDSTONE CHANGES COLOR AT NIGHT!

ULURU
AKA AYERS ROCK

ALICE SPRINGS
THE HEART AND SOUL OF THE OUTBACK

AUSTRALIA

SYDNEY

VICTORIA

CAMP BILLABONG!

AUSTRALIA AND NEW ZEALAND ARE ABOUT 380 MILES AWAY FROM EACH OTHER

MELBOURNE

PORT PHILLIP BAY
THE HIDING PLACE OF BLOODY BONITO'S TREASURE!

NEW ZEALAND

QUICK NOTE FROM BICK KIDD

G'day, mates!

Before we begin our awesome adventure in the land of Oz (which is what some people call Australia), I just wanted to remind everybody that I, Bickford "Bick" Kidd, will be your fair dinkum journo, which means I'll be writing the story while my twin sister, Rebecca "Beck" Kidd, a ridgy-didge, bobby-dazzler of a doodler, will be drawing the illustrations.

And, before we're done, you might even learn what those Aussie slang words mean.

But first, we have some treasure to hunt!

PART ONE

THE WONDERS DOWN UNDER

CHAPTER 1

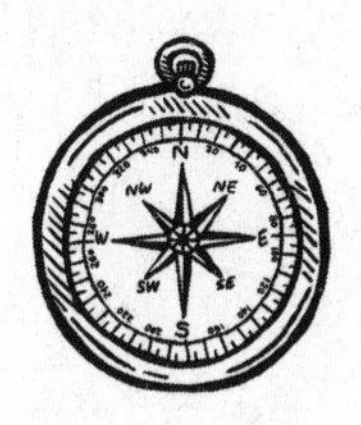

You know what's between the Hawaiian Islands and the island continent of Australia?

Water!

Lots and lots of water. Half an ocean of the salty, seaweedy stuff.

We were sailing the whole way because Mom and Dad had promised us that we Kidds would one day, before we grow up, explore every single continent on the planet. Once we do Australia, we'll only have Antarctica left, although I'm not sure what kind of treasure we could dig up down in penguin land. Maybe a pirate ice chest filled with Popsicles.

Uncle Richie "Poppie" Luccio was also with us on board *The Lost,* which, I know, is not the best name for a boat, especially when you're sailing across an ocean that covers more than sixty million square miles. That's a lot of deep and square miles to get lost in.

You might remember Uncle Richie from our last adventure back home in the USA. He helped Beck, Storm, Tommy, and me track down some long-lost American treasures while also helping us make sure the land of the free and the home of the brave stayed that way. *FREE.*

Uncle Richie is Mom's favorite uncle. He took her on her first archaeological dig way back when she was younger than Beck and me (we're twelve). He's a swaggering, blustery guy who'll probably remind you of Teddy Roosevelt (not that you've ever met Teddy Roosevelt, but you know what I mean).

"Land, ho!" shouted Storm from her perch up in the bow. "It's the coast of Tonga! I recognize its volcanic peaks."

Of course she did. Our big sister Storm has what they call a photographic memory. Once she sees something (like a topographical map of the coastline of Tonga, a Polynesian country east of New Zealand), she never forgets it.

"Bully, Storm!" shouted Uncle Richie. "Always keep your eyes on the stars and your feet on the ground!"

"It's daytime, Uncle Richie," Storm shouted back. "There aren't any stars. No ground, either. This is a boat."

"Ah, a very keen observation, Storm. Bully for you! Bully, I say."

"Bring her about, Tommy!" Dad shouted. Tommy, the oldest Kidd kid, was manning the wheel and letting the wind blow through his wavy hair—just in case any mermaids were checking him out, I guess.

"Drop anchor, Bick and Beck!" cried Mom. "Then we need to do our pre-dive prep protocol."

"Aye, aye," Beck and I shouted back. Actually, it was more like "aye, aye, aye, aye," since there's two of us.

It was time to climb into our wet suits and put on our SCUBA gear.

We were going on a dive. There was a ship just off the coast of Tonga. A vessel called the *Port Au Prince.*

Only it was *under* the water.

That's right. It was a shipwreck. And, legend had it, it was filled with treasure!

CHAPTER 2

We dropped anchor and pulled on our wet suits.

Well, everybody except Storm and Uncle Richie. Neither one really liked getting wet. They were kind of like cats that way. Sort of made the whole seafaring, oceangoing thing a little tricky for them.

"We shall remain on board and guard the treasures that this noble vessel already holds," Uncle Richie proclaimed dramatically, pointing one finger toward the sky.

"We'll probably also fix ourselves a sandwich," added Storm.

"Indeed," said Uncle Richie. "Tuna on rye might be nice."

As we dug out our SCUBA gear, Storm gave us a quick lesson on the *Port Au Prince* shipwreck. "It was a British privateer," she said.

"Cool," said Tommy. "Pirate ships are always loaded down with pirate booty—and not the salty, cheesy kind they sell in supermarkets."

"Privateer ships are different from pirate ships, Tommy," Storm explained. "The *Port Au Prince* was a private ship with a special commission from the English crown that gave it permission to attack and plunder the ships of Britain's rivals, Spain and France."

Dad picked up the story. He has a much more dramatic way of dishing out the facts. "And so, the *Port Au Prince* entered Tongan waters in 1806 in search of whales for whale oil, a prized commodity at the time. However, the ship was quickly seized by the local chief, Finau Ulukalala the second, whose warriors massacred most of the crew, including the captain, and then scuttled the vessel, with all the treasure still on board."

"That means there's a vast amount of copper, silver, and gold resting with the wreck on the bottom of the sea," said Storm. "Not to mention a number of silver candlesticks, jewel-encrusted crucifixes, and gold chalices."

"Woo-hoo," shouted Tommy, flapping across the deck in his flippers. "Let's do this thing."

As always, Tommy was the first one ready to dive.

"Buddy up," said Mom. "Go through your pre-dive checklist."

Beck and I checked out each other's equipment, using the BWRAF technique Mom and Dad taught us when we were toddlers. No, BWRAF is not the noise people make when they barf. It means you check for Buoyancy, Weights, Releases, Air, then you do a Final okay: inspecting the fins, mask, and snorkel, checking out our dive flashlights, taking a compass bearing, and giving Mom and Dad a gloved thumbs-up.

While Beck and I BWARFed each other, Mom, Dad, and Tommy checked one another out, too.

"We are good to go!" Dad pronounced. "Remember, it's even more important that we all stick together down below."

He popped his regulator into his mouth and lowered his mask. We all did the same. Then Dad and Tommy scissor-kicked off the back of the boat while Beck, Mom, and I went with the backward flop over the side. It's like an upside-down cannonball dive. It's way cooler than just flicking your flippers as you step off the boat.

We regrouped underwater. Dad consulted the dive computer in his watch and made a series of hand gestures telling us which way to kick and swim.

The five of us were like a well-organized school of fish, following Dad down into an amazing world of pink and orange reefs where brilliant little red and blue fish seemed to glow as they darted in and out of the coral formations.

But then something shiny caught my eye.

A glint of silver.

Dad kept leading us onward.

Which meant the shimmering object was soon *behind* us.

I looked over to Beck. She'd seen the silvery glint, too.

We also both simultaneously knew the terrible truth: Dad's dive computer had messed up.

It was leading us *away* from the sunken treasure!

CHAPTER 3

Beck and I kicked our flippers into high gear.

We were bringing up the rear of the dive pack but we needed to catch up with Dad to let him know that he and his super sophisticated dive watch were swimming the wrong way.

That's when a humpback whale came between Beck and me and the rest of our dive team. It slid right in front of us. We had to slam on the brakes and let it pass.

When the Big Bad Whale finally swam on by, Mom, Dad, and Tommy were about fifty yards away. They didn't see the whale cross behind

them because SCUBA masks don't come with rearview mirrors. They also weren't looking over their shoulders to see how Beck and I were doing. They assumed we were still obeying Dad's orders, sticking with the pack, and bringing up the rear.

I swerved around and hand signaled to Beck. When you're on a dive, that's just about the only way to communicate. You can't talk into an underwater walkie-talkie because your mouth is already busy breathing. Over the years, Beck and I have developed a few Twins Only hand gestures that go well beyond the usual stuff for "Okay," "Level off," and "Ears won't clear."

"We should go back to where we saw the sparkle!" I signaled. For "sparkle," I popped my fingers wide open on both hands like a Broadway dancer.

"We should stay with the group!" Beck signaled back.

"And abandon the treasure? You're nuttier than a squirrel's cheeks!" That one involved me twirling fingers near my temples while making a chubby-cheeked, buck-toothed face behind my mask.

"Oh, yeah?" Beck signaled back. "You're nuttier than a pecan pie on the Fourth of July." I think that's what her rapid series of gestures meant.

And just like that, we erupted into our first ever underwater Twin Tirade.

When we have TTs on dry land, we both erupt with volcanic fury, spew molten lava at each other, and then, after a few good blasts of hot, fiery gas, cool off instantly—just like lava when it

WE NEED TO GET BACK!
YOU NEED BETTER PERSONAL HYGIENE.
YOU CAN'T SMELL ME UNDERWATER! YOU'RE WEARING A MASK!
I KNOW. IT'S WHY I LIKE TO DIVE SO MUCH.
I LIKE DIVING, TOO.
SO WHAT ARE WE ARGUING ABOUT?
THE TREASURE. WE SHOULD GO BACK AND GET IT.
WELL, DUH. WE'RE TREASURE HUNTERS. GOING FOR TREASURE IS WHAT WE DO.
WE'RE COOL?
NEVER BETTER. NOW LET'S GO PICK UP THAT SILVERWARE BACK THERE.

slides into the ocean, simmers down, and makes a brand-new island for an archipelago.

After about fifteen seconds of rapid-fire hand and arm gestures, our subaquatic Twin Tirade was over.

Beck and I decided to go semi-rogue and retrieve the treasure from the spot we'd passed over earlier. We figured Mom and Dad would forgive us once we showed them how they'd swum right past the shipwreck without seeing it. Beck and I are younger than Mom, Dad, and Tommy. That means our eyesight is sharper.

We swam back to where we'd seen the silvery glint.

We saw it again!

And soon realized it was just a fish. A dogtooth tuna, I believe. They're very silvery. They're also very common in the tropical waters of the Pacific Ocean.

Beck gave me a look of frustration.

I shrugged my shoulders.

I was about to signal, "Let's head back to the

others" when something slimy wrapped around my legs and waist.

Turned out, it was the same thing that was grabbing Beck's arms.

A giant octopus!

CHAPTER 4

And it wasn't just any octopus!

This was a massive eight-tentacled monster. A giant sea creature straight out of Greek, or in this case, Polynesian mythology. It latched on to Beck and me and wouldn't let go.

One of the octopus's suction-cupped appendages was squeezing my neck and cutting off my oxygen flow. I couldn't breathe, which is a horrible thing to have happen underwater (or anywhere, actually). Beck's face was turning green. Probably because the demented sea creature had her in his grip and was whipping her up and down as if she were a yo-yo in a wet suit.

I was about to close my eyes and say buh-bye when, all of a sudden, I could breathe again. Oxygen was flowing through my hoses and into my lungs.

Beck wasn't bobbing up and down anymore, either.

Because Tommy had swum to our rescue.

He was wrestling, as best he could, against the eight-armed underwater ninja. Good thing Mom and Dad taught us martial arts. Tommy was giving almost as good as he was getting. Too bad he only had four limbs to fight with.

Mom and Dad came churning through the water. Dad had his speargun raised! I noticed something odd on the tip: a ginormous seashell.

Dad aimed his weapon—away from the octopus—and fired!

The sea monster saw the shell go shooting by and, figuring it must be dinner, let go of Tommy and went jetting off after the flying shell.

I could see Dad's eyes, magnified by the lens of his dive mask. There was a mixture of anger and relief in them. He was mad at us for breaking away from the group, but glad we were all still alive.

I glanced over at Mom. She had the same set of emotions in her eyes. But, I think the anger took over once the octopus was safely away. She gave us one (and only one) hand gesture.

"Up!"

The five of us kicked hard and streaked back to the surface, as quickly as we could without giving ourselves decompression sickness or what they call "the bends."

We all scrambled up onto the boat. Mom and Dad insisted that Beck and I climb aboard first, then Tommy, then Dad, then Mom (Mom's the best swimmer in the whole family).

Once we'd ripped off our masks and regulators and caught our breath, Mom and Dad marched over to have "a word" with Beck and me. They had The Look. You've probably seen it. Right before your parents have "a word" with you.

"What did we say about sticking together down below?" asked Dad.

"That it's more important underwater than it is up here," said Mom, answering for us. That was fine with Beck and me. We were really dreading this particular pop quiz.

"Explain yourselves," said Dad.

"W-w-well," I stammered, "we saw this shiny, silvery object."

"It turned out to be a fish," added Beck.

"But first there was this whale," I said. "It cut us off from you guys."

"Was it silver, too?" asked Tommy, strutting across the deck, drying his hair with a towel, giving his mane a good shake, looking like he lived in a shampoo commercial.

"No," said Beck. "It was more blue."

Uncle Richie and Storm came up from the galley. They both had toast crumbs sprinkled across their shirts.

"Is everything all right?" asked Uncle Richie.

"Fine," said Mom. "Now."

"But Bick and Beck went totally rogue on us down below," said Tommy. "Thought they could fly solo, treasure hunt alone."

Uncle Richie shook his head and clamped one hand on each of our shoulders. "Bickford? Rebecca? If I may?"

We nodded. We could tell he wanted to give us some wise advice. It's what he likes to do. Who were we to try and stop him?

"Always remember one thing, children." Uncle Richie stiffened his spine and planted his fists on his hips. "Alone we can do so little; together we can do so much!"

"Chya," said Tommy. "Like, together, we can save Bick and Beck's butts. Repeatedly."

Dad chuckled. "We can also find a certain privateer's treasure."

He held up a single black coin and rubbed it clean with his thumb. With the oxidation scraped off, the coin revealed itself to be silver. It sparkled and shimmered in the sun—way more than that tuna fish Beck and I went chasing after.

CHAPTER 5

Seems Mom, Dad, and Tommy had found the sunken *Port Au Prince* (exactly where Dad's dive computer said it would be) but had to scurry away from the shipwreck with only one silver coin when they saw Beck and me tangled up in a tango with an eight-legged monster.

"Everybody recheck their gear," said Dad. "We're going back down. Let's grab the metal detectors and dive nets."

"This is going to be quite a haul," said Mom. "On first inspection, the cargo hold looked to be loaded with treasure chests."

"Woo-hoo!" shouted Tommy. "We're gonna be rich."

"Actually, Thomas," said Dad, "we already have more money than we'll ever need."

"Even if, someday, I want to buy, like, a Maserati or a Lamborghini?"

"You can buy those with your own money, Tommy," said Mom. "Any treasure we find down below will be immediately donated to the Tonga National Museum in Nuku'alofa."

"But then we're heading on to Australia to search for Lasseter's Gold," I said. "Right?"

"Indeed, we are," said Uncle Richie, getting kind of wound up. "For it is the stuff of myth and legend! The most famous of all of Australia's long-lost treasures. Imagine, an inland reef, hidden in the desert, rich with gold."

Tommy raised his hand.

"Yes, Tommy?" said Mom.

"Are we gonna donate all of Lasseter's Gold to a museum when we find it?"

"We will give it to whomever deserves it," said Dad.

"Fine," said Tommy, sounding sort of sullen. "Whatever."

I think he really wanted to buy a snazzy car.

"First things first," said Mom. "Before we head off to Australia ..."

"Which is still three thousand two hundred and thirty-nine miles away," added Storm.

"Thank you, Stephanie," said Mom, who, by the way, is one of the few people allowed to call Storm by her real name. Dad and Uncle Richie are the other two. "Before we even think about Australia and Lasseter's Gold, we need to retrieve the *Port Au Prince*'s silver and jewels!"

So, we all went through our pre-dive checks once again and grabbed the extra gear we'd need for finding and then hauling the treasure up to the surface. We tumbled and scissor-kicked back into the ocean. This time, Beck and I were behind Mom and Dad but in front of Tommy. When I glanced over my shoulder, he did one of those two fingers to his eyes, two fingers to me, two fingers back to his eyes gestures. Yep. He would be watching us.

Hauling treasure out of a sunken hull is always a blast.

We use a metal detector to sweep the

barnacle-encrusted wreckage to make sure we don't miss anything. Then we load dive nets with as much loot as they can hold.

Working together, we had five big bags stuffed with silver candlesticks, gold crosses, and jeweled goblets. The museum in Tonga would probably need a new wing to house it all.

Mom gave the signal and we headed back up, dragging our bulging treasure nets behind us. When we broke through the surface of the water, we noticed something peculiar.

Another boat was docked right next to ours. *The Venus* was stenciled across its stern. From our vantage point, bobbing up and down in the water, we could see Uncle Richie and Storm chatting with a giant of a woman. She had to be six feet tall with long blond dreadlocks streaming out of her wide red bandana. Even though the sun was scorching hot, she wore a waxy-looking long coat and boots up to her knees. Two men, with muscles nearly as thick and big as hers, were standing beside her. The lady looked like an Amazon warrior. And not the kind that sells things online.

VENUS. GODDESS OF LOVE. THAT MUST BE THE LOVE BOAT.
THE VENUS

CHAPTER 6

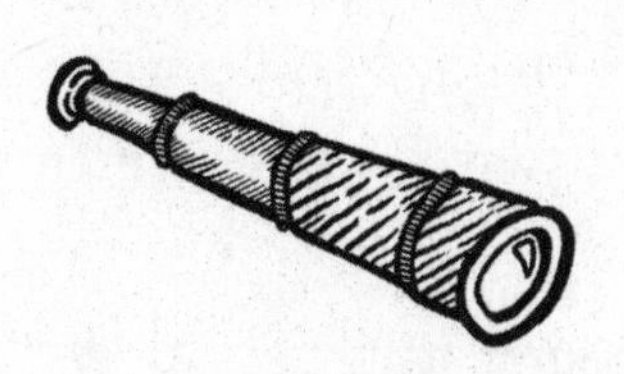

Tommy was open-mouth gawking at the lady who had to be at least ten years older than him.

"I think I'm in love," he blubbered.

In case you didn't know, Tommy falls head over heels in love on a regular basis. It's why Mom and Dad nicknamed him Tailspin Tommy.

He started swimming for our ship, faster than I've ever seen him swim before—even though he was hauling two heavy, treasure-filled dive bags behind him. The guy moved like a torpedo slicing through the waves.

Yep. He was definitely tailspinning again.

Beck and I swam after him. So did Mom and

Dad. But Tommy beat us all to the dive ladder, clambered up, dumped his treasure bags on the deck, and tried his best to look suave and cool, which is kind of hard to do when you're dressed like a frogman with an oxygen tank strapped to your back.

"Hey," I heard him say to the lady when we were all back on deck. "I'm Tommy. And you must be . . . gorgeous!"

Storm rolled her eyes. Beck did her famous "gag me now" gesture. Mom and Dad both shook

their heads. We were all kind of used to Tommy and his tailspinning.

Fortunately, the lady laughed. A big, boisterous laugh. Uncle Richie joined in. Then the two big guys behind the lady laughed, too.

"G'day to you, Tommy," said the lady. "I'm Charlotte Badger. These are my mates from down under, Banjo and Croc."

"G'day," said the two men, who had very stubbly beards, lots of piercings, and more arm tattoos than a Maori warrior.

"Ms. Badger and her esteemed associates hail from Australia," said Uncle Richie. "They might be able to offer us invaluable assistance in our quest for Lasseter's Gold."

"Be happy to help, mate," said Ms. Badger.

"Bully!"

I'm not sure if Uncle Richie was supposed to be discussing our Australian treasure hunt with total strangers. But it was our main mission. And if the lady was from Australia, she might be able to help us find one of the biggest missing treasures in the whole world: Lasseter's Gold!

"I see you lot already beat us to the *Port Au Prince*," said the lady, gesturing to dive nets loaded with clinking treasure we'd flung up on the deck. "Good on you. You did a bonzer job. My mates and I do a wee bit of treasure hunting ourselves from time to time. But you beat us to this beaut, fair and square."

"I'm Dr. Thomas Kidd," said Dad, stepping forward to shake Ms. Badger's hand. "I take it you've already met Storm and Uncle Richie."

"We've yabbered. They're both bobby-dazzlers."

"Well, this is my wife Sue. Our twins, Beck and Bick. And, of course, our oldest, Thomas."

Tommy wiggle-waggled his eyebrows. "I think I just found all the treasure I'll ever need," he said to Ms. Badger. "You!"

Ms. Badger boomed up another big laugh. Banjo and Croc echoed it.

"Ripper!" she said. "You're a fair dinkum dag, aren't you, now?"

"Huh?" said Tommy.

"A genuine funny fellow," Ms. Badger explained. "You're also kind of cute."

She winked at Tommy. He actually blushed.

Ms. Badger squinted up at the sun. "Cooee. Comin' on a scorcher. Mind if we head below-decks? If you have a map of the Aussie Outback, I can give you some ridgy-didge intel on where Lasseter's buried reef of solid gold might be."

"Ridgy-didge means genuine, authentic, or true," said Storm, who'd probably spent our dive time memorizing an Australian slang dictionary.

"Well," said Dad. "We already—"

"Let's go down below!" said Tommy, cutting Dad off. "We can show you The Room, too!"

"Thomas?" said Mom, shaking her head.

Tommy acted like he didn't hear Mom or see the way Dad was frowning at him.

"Oooh," purred Ms. Badger. "What's in 'the room,' Tommy?"

"All sorts of super-cool stuff. It's like a floating treasure museum!"

It's also filled with top-secret stuff—like charts and treasure maps and highly classified research that Mom, Dad, and Storm do to plot our quests. The Room was where they figured out how to pinpoint the *Port Au Prince*. Everything in The Room is usually protected by The Door, a heavy-duty bank vault–type thing made out of thick steel, and sealed by The Lock, which you can only open if you have The Key.

Yes, everything about The Room is spoken about in capital letters. It's that high security.

And now Tommy wanted to show it off to a perfect stranger, just because she was pretty?

"Come on, Charlotte," he said. "Right this way."

Of course he did.

CHAPTER 7

Have you ever fast-cleaned your room in the fifteen seconds you had before your parents stepped through the door?

That's what Mom and Dad did. They hurried down belowdecks before anybody else and told Tommy to make sure he showed Ms. Badger "his incredible hiding place" in the galley.

So, Tommy showed Ms. Badger the secret compartment he built for stashing his hot sauce collection.

"See? You tap this pine knot, a cabinet door flips open, and there's my Tapatío, my Jamaican, my Frank's RedHot, and, of course, my El Yucateco Green Habanero."

That slight side trip bought Mom and Dad just enough time to toss blankets and towels and sheets and foul weather gear over whatever they didn't want an outsider to see in The Room. They even spun around the corkboards cluttered with pinned-up papers and charts and maps and aerial photographs for our upcoming Australian adventure. The back sides linked together like a block puzzle to create a decorative mural: an innocent image of a friendly mermaid swimming with an even friendlier dolphin.

When Tommy and Charlotte finally drifted into The Room, followed by me, Beck, Storm, and Uncle Richie, all anybody could see was that mural and a couple of display cases filled with art, artifacts, and antiquities.

"And right there," said Tommy, proudly pointing to the cabinets, "you can see some of the treasure junk we've found over the years. That's a conquistador helmet. We think it used to belong to a conquistador."

"Impressive, mate," said Charlotte with a whistle.

"Yeah," said Tommy, picking up a heavy jade Buddha statue. He curled it as if it were a dumbbell. His biceps bulged. "A lot of the ladies say that about me."

"What's this one here?" Charlotte picked up an empty jar.

"Careful," urged Mom, trying her best to smile. "That's a rare piece of pre-Columbian pottery."

"Coo. I like this brass incense burner, too," said Charlotte, putting down the clay pot and hoisting the next treasure out of its display case.

"It's shaped like a Hindu goddess," said Beck.

"Just like you," Tommy said to Charlotte. Then he wiggled his eyebrows some more.

Charlotte Badger laughed. "Crikey, you're a right bosker bloke, Tommy." She put the incense burner back in its cabinet. "Now then, let's talk about Lasseter's Gold. Australia's most prized and elusive treasure."

"Bully!" said Uncle Richie. "Such is this family's current quest. What can you tell us about it, Ms. Badger?"

"Only this," said the powerfully built, towering

woman (she had to duck down a little to keep her dreadlocks from scraping the ceiling). "You'd have to be barmy as a bandicoot to go lookin' for it. A real ningnong."

We all looked to Storm. She translated: "We'd be nuts to try and find it."

"Why?" I asked.

"First off," said Ms. Badger, "it's probably just a legend made up by a dipstick who couldn't give cheese away at a rat's birthday party. Second, if it does exist, it's situated in the sweltering Outback where it's so blistering hot the crows fly backward to keep the sun out of their eyes."

"Um, is there a third reason we shouldn't go?" I asked squeamishly.

"Too right. In fact, it's the most important reason of them all."

"What is it?" asked Tommy, his eyes widening.

Charlotte Badger jabbed a thumb toward the ceiling. "Me and my mates, Banjo and Croc, will find it long before you lot ever do."

"Excuse me?" said Dad.

"I told you, old man," said Ms. Badger, with

a laugh. "We're treasure hunters. Oh, sure, you might've beaten us to the *Port Au Prince* here in Tonga but you'll never beat us back home in Oz."

Dad narrowed his eyes. "What makes you say that?"

Ms. Badger grinned. It wasn't a pretty one. "Oh, you'll find out soon enough, Dr. Kidd."

She started backing up toward The Door. Tommy, who was the closest, might've been able to grab her and stop her from escaping but he was too busy being heartbroken.

"You know," Ms. Badger taunted, "for being so world famous, you Kidds sure are a dim lot. I've seen better heads on mugs of root beer. Word to the not-so-wise? Never leave two unattended pirates up on your deck while their pirate captain lures you down below—away from your sails and rigging."

"You're a pirate?" gasped Tommy.

"Aye, that I am." She pulled a very long, very scary knife out of her duster coat. It was almost as long as a pirate's swashbuckling sword.

She tossed back her head and laughed heartily.

Then she spun around, took strides the size of kangaroo hops, bounded out of The Room, dashed through the galley, and scrambled back up to the deck.

Beck and I raced after her.

When we scampered topside, we could hear her ship, *The Venus,* motoring away.

We could also hear our mainsail flapping in the breeze like a line of plastic pennants at a used car lot.

While we'd been downstairs, showing Ms. Badger Tommy's hot sauce collection and a few of our favorite artifacts, Ms. Badger's pirate buddies, Banjo and Croc, had cut our mainsail to shreds with knives and daggers that were probably even longer than hers.

SO LONG, YOU MOPOKES*! YOU'RE REALLY IN THE POO** NOW!
* IDIOTS
** IN TROUBLE
THE VENUS

CHAPTER 8

For a second, we all stood on deck, just staring up at our tattered sails as they snapped and flapped in the South Pacific breeze.

"This is all my fault!" said Tommy. "Again. How many times have I fallen for a pretty girl only to have her turn out to be some sort of nefarious spy or bad actor?"

"At least seven," I said.

"Are you counting that Russian lady?" asked Beck.

"Oh, right. Forgot her. Probably eight. Maybe nine."

Storm, who, of course, would know the precise

number of femmes fatales that Tommy had been tricked by in our adventures, remained silent. Instead, she put a comforting hand on his shoulder and said, "Tommy, the only man who never makes a mistake is the man who never does anything."

"Bully for you, Storm!" cried Uncle Richie. "You memorized that book of Teddy Roosevelt motivational quotes I gave you."

"She tricked us all, Thomas," said Dad, clamping his hand on Tommy's free shoulder.

"We knew the risks," added Mom. "But your father and I thought Ms. Badger might be able to give us valuable information about the Outback."

"Instead," I cracked, "she played with our valuable treasures down below so her pirate pals could do incredible damage up here."

"And," said Uncle Richie, "if I may offer an observation, I believe Ms. Badger's true intention was to damage more than the fabric in our mainsail, spinnaker, and jib. No, friends. I believe she intended to rip apart the fabric that holds this family together. If we're bickering and blaming one another, then we can't be pulling together to chase after her!"

"Chya," said Tommy, a fiery light returning to his eyes. "Well, that's not gonna happen, Uncle Richie. We're gonna beat her to Australia! Then, after that, we're gonna beat her to Lasseter's Gold!"

"That's the spirit, Thomas!" shouted Uncle Richie.

"Hear, hear!" echoed Mom, Dad, and Storm.

Beck and I were still a little skeptical.

"Um, exactly how are we going to do that?" I wondered aloud. "Our sailboat doesn't have any sails."

"So, what?" said Tommy. "*The Lost* can perform under sail *or* under power. If we tweak out the engines, maybe improvise a turbocharger, we can outrun that hunk of junk pirate ship. Dad, we should also check the compression valves and adjust our propeller height."

"Of course," said Dad. "Good thinking, Thomas!"

Storm nodded. "Raising the drives higher out of the water will improve speed because it will reduce drag."

"And," said Mom, "we have spare sails hidden in several secret compartments."

"Then what are we waiting for?" said Tommy, suddenly sounding like the ship captain he was born to be. "I want the engines tweaked, the propellers raised, and new sails rigged and ready to run in twenty minutes."

"Twenty?" I said, totally pumped by Tommy's pep talk. "We can do it in fifteen!"

"Nah," said Tommy, shooting me a wink. "We should give Charlotte Badger a head start. It's only fair. She doesn't know who she's up against! We're the Kidds."

"Boo-yah!" I said. Then Beck and I knocked knuckles. We also floss-danced a little.

And then we went to work.

We rigged the sails with Mom and Storm.

Dad, Tommy, and Uncle Richie fiddled with the engines.

Twenty minutes later, we were ready to blast off. We still had three thousand miles of ocean to cross before we'd hit the port of Sydney, Australia. Traveling at about 26.8 knots (or 30.8 miles per hour), that meant it would take us maybe one hundred hours or 4.1666666 days. Yes, sometimes math comes in very handy, especially on a ship.

And on the morning of the fourth day, guess who we passed just as we cruised into Australia's Sydney harbour?

That's right.

Charlotte Badger and *The Venus*.

Those scurvy, cheating pirates never had a chance up against us Kidds!

CHAPTER 9

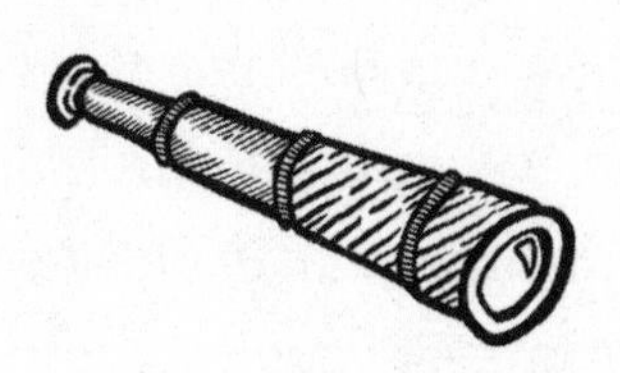

"Hoist the Q-flag, Bick," said Dad as we pulled into the port.

"Aye, aye!" I grabbed the yellow flag out of our crate of international maritime signal flags. I wasn't sure why Dad was going with "Q" to celebrate our arrival in Sydney. Maybe because Australia has a state called Queensland. Or maybe because sailing at 30.8 miles per hour for four days across choppy waters will make anybody Queasy.

"We are requesting a pratique," Dad explained as I ran the yellow flag up its line. "Since this vessel is sailing under an American flag, we need to convince the Australian authorities that our ship is free from any contagious diseases."

"Several human and plant diseases have never reached these shores," added Storm, our walking-talking Wikipedia. "It's why Australia is home to the most vigilant quarantine officers in the world. They board every aircraft landing in Australia and spray the cabin air with insecticide and disinfectant. They won't let you bring any food, animals, plants, or soil into the country."

"Seriously?" said Tommy. "Because I still have half a microwaved cheeseburger down in the galley and some potato chips ..."

"They call them potato crisps in Australia," said Storm.

"So? I bought them in Hawaii."

"Good point."

"Wait a second," said Beck, as Tommy eased back on the throttles. "Charlotte Badger is flying an Australian flag. Her ship won't have to go through the whole quarantine thing!"

"Right you are, Beck," said Dad. "I'm afraid our current lead in this treasure hunt might soon be erased."

And it was.

A customs boat, a unit of the Australian Border Force, saw our yellow flag and came out to meet us in the harbor.

"Welcome to Australia, Kidd Family Treasure Hunters," said the very proper customs captain as he boarded *The Lost*. He was a very serious looking man with no hair and no smile.

Turns out, Dad had notified the authorities

about our arrival weeks ago, when we first set sail from Hawaii. But the paperwork and inspection were going to take a ton of time. They wanted our passports, visas, and all sorts of information about where we'd been, who we were, did we have any animals on board (yes, Beck almost told them I was a pig), and were we carrying any firearms. That led to some awkward reveals from hidden cupboards scattered around the ship. When you sail through pirate-infested waters, you need to pack a few defensive weapons.

"You'll need to leave those weapons sealed on board during your stay in Australia," said the customs officer. "Even the crossbow. Now, then, we need to spray all cabins belowdecks with insecticide and disinfectant. We will also need to destroy any open food."

He motioned for some of his crew to start inspecting the cabins belowdecks.

"There goes my cheeseburger," mumbled Tommy.

"You folks, of course, are required to stay on board your ship for twenty-four hours."

"What?" said Tommy. "That's like a whole day!"

"Too right," said the officer. Then he pointed to the Q-flag overhead. "That's why we call it a quarantine."

"Hang on," Tommy said to the captain of the customs boat. "This quarantine dealio will give Charlotte Badger a whole day's jump on us."

"Excuse me?"

"Charlotte Badger," I explained. "She's a treasure hunter like us."

"She's also a pirate," blurted Beck.

"Right you are," said the customs agent. "Charlotte Badger was the most notorious lady pirate in all of Australian history. However, if memory serves, she died in 1816."

We all looked at Storm.

"I have a photographic memory, you guys," she said defensively. "That doesn't mean I know everything. Just what I've seen, read, or memorized."

"Of course it doesn't, Storm," said Uncle Richie. "I imagine our Charlotte Badger is only using that famous pirate name as an alias."

"We need to catch her," said Beck. "We can't waste time just sitting here in the harbor."

"The law is the law, Rebecca," said Dad. "We'll just have to make up for the lost time once we've cleared customs."

"We can do it," said Mom.

"We can do anything we set our mind to," added Uncle Richie. "Once on dry land, let us strive mightily. For I would rather run the risk of wearing out than rusting out!"

"Bully!" shouted Storm. She and Uncle Richie were kind of kindred spirits.

One of the customs agents, a lady who'd gone down below to search and spray our cabins, came back up to the deck holding a white paper bag in her rubber-gloved hand.

"Chief?" she said to the captain. "I found something."

"My cheeseburger?" said Tommy.

The agent shook her head. "No, mate. This is much more valuable. It's also much more stolen."

CHAPTER 10

"What'd you find, Charlie?" the captain asked his officer.

"One of the missing Lightning Ridge Opals," replied the officer, opening the top of the white paper sack so her boss could take a peek inside.

"Crikey," said the captain, looking and sounding amazed. "Call me a cough drop if that's not the Black Prince of the Inland Sea. All one-hundred-and-eighty-one carats in a three-inch by two-inch stone."

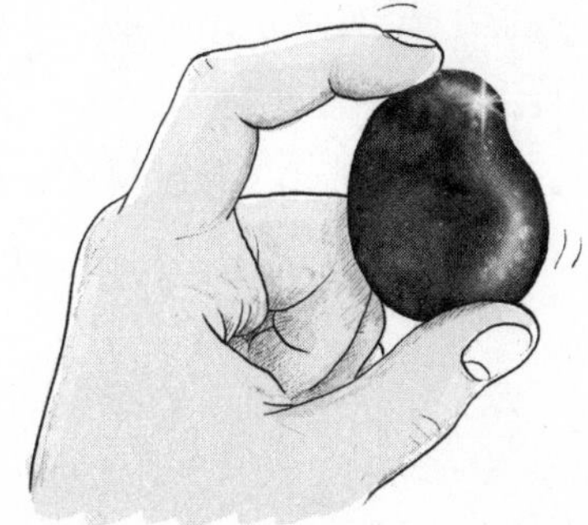

THIS STONE HAS MORE CARATS THAN BUGS BUNNY.

"Black opals typically sell for fifteen thousand Australian dollars per carat," said Storm, who knows stuff like that even if she doesn't know all the Famous Pirates of Australia.

"Whoa," said Tommy. "That means that little rock is worth . . . a lot of money."

"Two million, seven-hundred-and-fifteen thousand Australian dollars," said Mom, who, of course, is our home school math instructor on board *The Lost*.

"Or one million, nine-hundred-and-sixty-five thousand US dollars," said Storm, who, in her free time, memorized currency conversion rates.

"This is just one of the missing stones," said the customs boat captain. "It was stolen with two even more valuable black opals."

"Where'd you find it?" Tommy asked eagerly.

"Down below," replied the customs officer. "In a cabin decorated with a mural of a mermaid swimming with a dolphin."

Beck and I looked at each other. She was talking about The Room.

"It was rattling around inside an antique clay pot," the officer continued.

"She put it there!" I shouted.

"Charlotte Badger!" said Beck. "Or whatever her real name is."

"That's right," I said. "She probably used some pirate's pickpocket-ish sleight-of-hand trick and plunked it into our piece of pre-Columbian pottery while she distracted us by fumbling around with the incense burner!"

"That makes sense!" said Beck.

"Thank you, sis."

"You're welcome, Bick. It happens so rarely, we need to celebrate it when it does."

The two customs agents were looking at each other with very serious expressions on their faces. The captain slowly re-examined our stack of passports.

"You are, of course, *the* Dr. Thomas and Susan Kidd?" he asked.

"Yes," said Dad.

"You're world-famous treasure hunters, correct?"

"We sure are," said Tommy. "We've even been on TV a couple times. We might start our own YouTube channel someday, too."

"Well, then," said the captain, rubbing his bald dome, "this is a bit of a sticky wicket."

"How so?" asked Dad.

"You're treasure hunters. That means you flit about the globe, hunting for treasure. Gold. Silver. Precious jewels. How'd you end up with one of the most famous opals in all of Australia?"

"As the children told you," said Mom, "we can only presume that Charlotte Badger, or whatever her real name is, planted it downstairs in that piece of pottery."

"I don't like presuming things," said the captain.

"Besides, why would she do that?" asked the officer who'd found the stone. "Why'd she deposit a two-million-dollar opal in your crockery?"

"To slow us down," said Uncle Richie. "You see, officers, we are in a bit of a race with Ms. Badger. We're both off to the Outback in search of

Lasseter's Lost Reef of Gold!"

"You plan on stealing that, too, mate?" asked the officer.

"We don't steal treasures!" said Dad.

The captain rattled the opal bag. "This little gem? It was stolen. Then we found it tucked away in one of your cabins."

"Sounds like stealing treasure to me," said Charlie, the officer.

"You only found it on our ship because that's where the pirate lady stashed it!" shouted Tommy.

"Right," said the captain. "So you all keep saying. But I notice from your passport stamps, that you three adults have all traveled to Australia before. In fact, Dr. and Mrs. Kidd, your last visit was in 2002. Correct?"

"So?" said Mom. "How is that significant?"

"2002 is when the Black Prince of the Inland Sea and the other two opals went missing. Tell you what—you two can skip the quarantine here on your ship. Detective Superintendent Jonathan Michael Ruggiere will want to chat with you both."

"And who is Detective Superintendent Ruggiere?" asked Mom.

"The officer who heads up the Lightning Ridge Opals case for the Australian Federal Police. Been at it for nearly twenty years now."

"The AFP is like America's FBI," said Storm, because that must've been another factoid rattling around in her ginormous brain.

"We also need to confiscate any computers you might have on board," said the captain.

"Why?" demanded Dad.

"They might contain evidence related to your theft of the black opals."

"For the last time, officer," said Mom, "we're not thieves."

"Right. You're 'treasure hunters.' Tomahto, tomato. The rest of you lot stay here. We'll be in touch."

His officers took all three of our laptops.

Then one slapped handcuffs on Mom and Dad's wrists!

"Congratulations, Dr. and Mrs. Kidd," said the

captain, sarcastically. "You're about to become prisoners in a country that started out as a penal colony!"

CHAPTER 11

"We should go bust them out of jail!" said Tommy, ten seconds after the customs boat with Mom and Dad aboard roared off to Sydney.

"I don't think these guys are going to let us," I said, pointing to a second customs boat that was cutting across the first boat's wake so it could come keep an eye on us—and the other ships flying yellow Q-flags.

"We're stuck here in quarantine for another twenty-two hours and forty-nine minutes," said Storm. "There's nothing we can do."

"We can call our lawyers!" I said.

"Bully," said Uncle Richie. "What's their number?"

"Um, I don't know..."

"I don't think Mom and Dad actually have, like, lawyer-lawyers," said Tommy. "You know, the way people always do in TV shows."

"They do have a lawyer in New York City," said Storm. "His name is Ken Joelson. But he only does wills and estate planning."

"Not the barrister you want when going up against the Australian equivalent of the FBI," said Uncle Richie. "We'll need to find someone local."

"Who should we call, Storm?" asked Tommy.

She shrugged. "Sorry. I haven't memorized the Sydney phone book. Yet. We're stuck. We should make the best of this bad situation."

"A grand suggestion, Storm," said Uncle Richie. "Turning lemons into lemonade and all that."

"Okay," said Beck. "So how exactly do we make this lemonade?"

"And what if we'd rather have limeade?" asked Tommy.

"Yeah," I said. "Or orange soda?"

"Well," said Storm, "we could do some sight-seeing."

"Seriously?" I said. "We're on a boat. In the bay."

"And right behind you, Bickford, is the Sydney Opera House. It was completed in 1973 after sixteen years of construction. Built on a large slab of granite on Bennelong Point here in the harbor, its shells are covered with white tiles that many say resemble sails on ships ..."

"I think it looks like a turtle traffic jam," said Tommy, who wasn't really enjoying our big sister's floating tour of the city where our parents had just been arrested.

"I'm going to make a few phone calls," said Uncle Richie, grabbing the ship's satellite phone and heading down to his cabin. "After all, I spent a good deal of time here in Australia a few years back. I still have friends. They may be able to help us out of this *sticky wicket*, as the surly gentleman from customs called it."

As he headed down the steps, Storm started regaling us with trivial factoids about the Sydney Harbour Bridge.

"The bridge was first opened in 1932. It contains six million hand-driven rivets. It's the world's largest steel arch bridge ..."

Tommy raised his hand.

"Yes, Tommy?" said Storm. "Question?"

"Yeah. How much longer 'til we're out of quarantine?"

Storm glanced at her watch. "Twenty-two hours and thirty-seven minutes."

"Oh-kay. Think I'll head down below and see if Uncle Richie needs help dialing his phone."

"We can help with that, too!" I said.

"Yeah!" said Beck. "Good idea, Tommy."

"You want to help, too?" I said to Storm. "You're good with numbers."

"The best," said Beck.

Storm sighed. "Sure. Fine. I can tell you guys more about Sydney tomorrow, when we're actually there."

"Grrrrreat," I said.

Because I knew the instant the customs squad let us off *The Lost,* we wouldn't have time to do any touristy stuff.

We'd be too busy springing Mom and Dad out of jail.

CHAPTER 12

The next day, around two o'clock, after exactly twenty-four hours, the customs officials told us we were "free to disembark and enter Australia."

Then they told us that our boat was being impounded.

"We'll keep it locked up at our dock," the officer manning the customs boat told us. "Part of our Criminal Assets Confiscation Program."

"Dude?" said Tommy, angrily. "We're not criminals!"

"Too right. So far, just your parents have been accused of criminal activity. Detective Superintendent Jonathan Michael Ruggiere might also need your 'treasure hunting' vessel for evidence when he files charges. From what I hear, your mum and dad could be looking at twenty years behind bars."

"And where exactly are Dr. and Mrs. Kidd right now?" asked Uncle Richie, planting his hands defiantly on his hips.

The officer mimicked his moves.

"At the Long Bay Correctional Complex, mate. Officially known as Her Majesty's Australian Prison Long Bay, or, you know, Long Bay."

And so, the second we set foot in Sydney, we hailed a taxi and headed off to the prison, which was only about fifteen kilometers south of the harbor.

"Visiting a prisoner?" the cabbie asked.

"Yeah," said Tommy, who was riding up front. "Two of them. Our mother and father."

"Strewth!" said the driver, sounding surprised. "Reckon that makes you lot orphans."

"No, it doesn't," I shouted from the backseat. "They won't be in jail long!"

"They're innocent!" added Beck.

"One hundred percent," said Uncle Richie.

The cabbie nodded. "I reckon most of the other prisoners at Long Bay will tell you the same thing."

"Those are the Royal Botanic Gardens," said Storm, pointing to the passing scenery and trying to change the subject. "Coming up on your right will be the Art Gallery of New South Wales ..."

Twenty minutes (and way too many landmarks) later, we arrived at the prison.

"Right this way," said the guard who signed us in. "Detective Superintendent Ruggiere is expecting you."

"He is?" said Uncle Richie. "How did he even know we were coming?"

The guard shrugged. "The old crumbly codger is clever that way."

We were ushered down a dank cinder-block hall to an interview room. Through the tiny, wire-mesh-and-glass window in the door, I could see

Mom and Dad sitting at a scarred wooden table with a withered old man who had three strands of greasy gray hair combed across the crown of his head. Mom and Dad were in orange prison jumpsuits. The old man was in a rumpled tweed suit that looked two sizes too big.

The guard rattled and rolled his key ring,

found the one he was looking for, and opened the door.

"Mom! Dad!" We all hurried into the room.

"Are you okay?"

"Did they hurt you?"

"How do we get you guys out of here?"

To tell you the truth, I don't remember who said what. We were all kind of talking at the same time.

CHAPTER 13

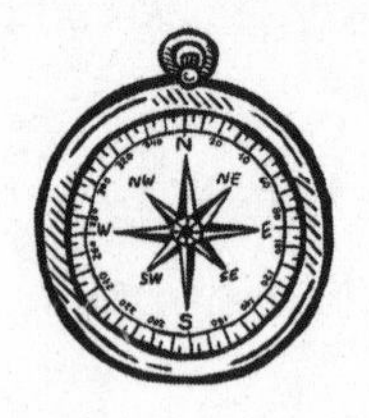

Mom and Dad smiled.

The old man looked at his watch. "Good on you. You took a taxi."

"Excuse me?" said Uncle Richie.

"Your ship's quarantine only ended forty-five minutes ago. It would take you ten minutes to be ferried from your impounded ship to the docks where, fortunately, you were able to hail a cab because it's not rush hour in Sydney. If you had taken the bus, we'd still be waiting for you."

"You guys?" said Mom. "This is Detective Superintendent Jonathan Michael Ruggiere."

"Please, call me Des."

"All right. Des here has been working the case of the missing Lightning Ridge Opals for two decades."

"Been trying to suss it out for twenty years," said the AFP detective. "Haven't had a fair dinkum clue or nibble for years. And then, crikey, your world-famous treasure-hunting parents turn up out of nowhere with one of my missing jewels rattling about in their pre-Columbian cookie jar."

"Because Charlotte Badger, which probably isn't her real name, dumped it there," said Tommy. "She wanted to slow us down. We're in, like, this major race to find Lasseter's Gold."

The old man nodded. "So I have been told."

"She's a pirate!" I shouted.

"Said so herself," added Beck.

"That's why she calls herself Charlotte Badger!" I yelled.

"She called her crewmates pirates, too," added Storm, who remembers everything. "Their names were Banjo and Croc. They had very distinctive tattoos and way too many nose- and earrings."

"Those names are probably made up, too,

Detective Des," suggested Tommy, trying to be helpful. "Unless, you know, one guy likes to play the banjo and the other one wrestles crocodiles or wears those goofy plastic shoes called Crocs…"

Now the detective looked confused. That happens sometimes when Tommy speaks. The detective held up a firm hand to silence all the yabbering.

"Perhaps what you children and your parents say is true," he announced. "However, the thief, or thieves, who stole the Black Prince of the Inland Sea also stole two other black opals that are even more valuable: The Pride of Australis and the Black Galaxy."

"Well, sir," I said, "your customs guys only found one opal on board our ship! Where are the other two? See? That proves we're not the thieves."

"Unless," muttered Storm, "we'd already sold the other ones."

"Oh, right. My bad. Forget I said that."

"I'll try, mate," said Detective Superintendent Ruggiere as he creaked back in his chair. "Ladies and gentlemen, boys and girls, I pride myself on being a reasonable bloke. However, I am also impatient and eager to retire. My wife wants to see your Grand Canyon. And Disneyland. I should've taken her there years ago but, well, I've been obsessed with hunting down the Lightning Ridge Opals. I can't just up and quit the Australian Federal Police without closing the one case that's been a boil on my bum for twenty years. Also, here in Australia, we believe in speedy trials. Especially when the lead investigator wants to retire and see Disneyland. So, I will make you treasure hunters a deal."

Uncle Richie rubbed his hands together, eagerly. He likes deals.

"Do go on, good sir," he said.

"If you four children and your elderly friend..."

"I'm their great-uncle Richie," he explained.

"He's Mom's uncle," I explained. "That's what makes him great. Well, that and the fact that he's pretty cool."

Uncle Richie nodded elegantly in my general direction. "Thank you, Bickford."

The detective started nervously fidgeting with

one of the hair strands clinging to his scalp. "So this truly is a family business, eh?"

"Yes, sir," said Dad. "It truly is."

"Very well," said the detective superintendent. "We will schedule Dr. and Mrs. Kidd's trial for one week from today. If you five assorted family members can bring me exculpatory evidence..."

"Huh?" said Tommy.

"That means evidence favorable to Mom and Dad," Storm explained.

"Precisely," said the detective. "If, within the week, you five can furnish me with the other two purloined opals as evidence exonerating your parents, I will gladly drop all charges, release your mother and father, and arrest this Charlotte Badger character. After seven days, however, I cannot help you. Because, my friends, I have already put in my retirement papers. These are my final seven days with the force. This time next week, it's, 'Hello, Disneyland.' You'll have to deal with whomever takes over my caseload. So, do we have a deal?"

"Bully!" cried Uncle Richie.

The detective looked confused again. "Is that a yes?"

"Definitely!" we all said together.

We hugged and kissed and said good-bye to Mom and Dad faster than we ever had.

Because the clock was ticking.

We only had seven days to catch the real opal thieves!

CHAPTER 14

We booked a bunch of rooms at a hotel right off Darling Harbour in the heart of Sydney.

"We'll only be staying one night," Uncle Richie told the clerk as we checked in.

We couldn't sleep on board *The Lost,* which was docked with the customs people. Our ship had been "impounded as evidence of high crimes on the high seas."

Since we were all kind of hungry and clagged out (another Australian phrase Storm taught us) after our exhausting afternoon, Uncle Richie suggested we head off to an early dinner at a nearby restaurant.

"We need to strategize," he said. "Something that's extremely difficult to do when you're so hungry you could eat a horse and chase the rider."

So, we went to a restaurant called Hunter and Barrel on Cockle Bay Wharf. There weren't many vegetarians in the place. The menu was full of stuff like beef skewers, crispy pork belly, and something called "eye of rump." (I don't even want to think of a buttocks with eyeballs. Neither does Beck.)

Tommy ordered the fried squid. Maybe because it reminded him of that octopus we tangled with off the coast of Tonga. Storm went with the hot cheese dip while Beck and I devoured a platter of crispy chicken wings. Uncle Richie had a cheeseburger. None of us wanted to even think about eating the second item on the "Fare Game" menu: Tasmanian kangaroo.

"We'll definitely want to try Vegemite while we're here," said Storm.

"What is it?" I made the mistake of asking.

"A thick, black food paste made from mashed yeast extract that you can spread on toast for breakfast."

BREAKFAST: THE MOST IMPORTANT AND, SOMETIMES, THE MOST DISGUSTING MEAL OF THE

Beck urped. “Sounds yummy,” she said.

“They even make a Vegemite smoothie,” said Storm.

“Bully,” said Uncle Richie. “Perfect for washing down some witchetty grubs.”

“What are *those*?” asked Tommy.

“Nutty-tasting little bugs. Actually, they are the wood-eating larvae of moths. Very crunchy.”

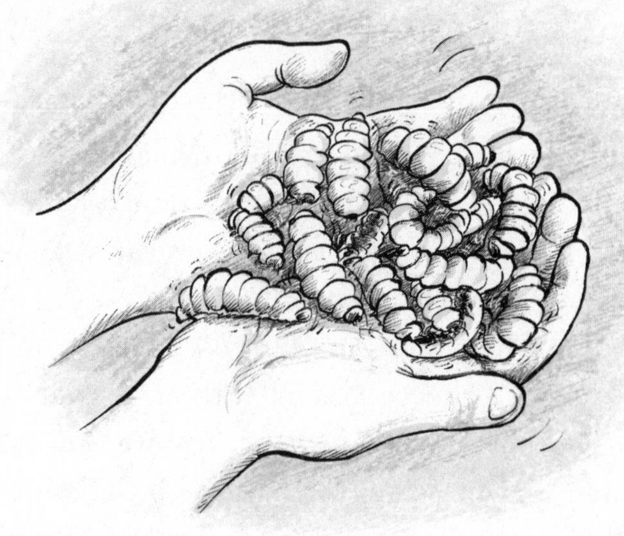

WITCHETTY GRUBS OR WIGGLY CHEETOS?

After that, none of us felt like ordering dessert.

We pushed away our plates and started hatching a plan.

“Storm?” asked Uncle Richie. “Did you by any chance memorize the maps and drawings pinned to the corkboards in The Room?”

“You mean the ones pinpointing what Mom and Dad both thought to be the precise location of Lasseter’s Gold?”

We all nodded.

"Well, duh," said Storm. "Of course I did."

"Excellent," cried Uncle Richie, giving the table a good silverware-rattling thump with both of his fists. "We must do what we can with what we have and where we are!"

"So where do we need to go?" I asked Storm.

"The Outback," said Storm. "The vast, remote interior of Australia. It's even more isolated and inaccessible than the bush, which is what Australians call anything that's not near a main population center. By the way, did you know that eighty-five percent of the Australian people live along the continent's coastline and within thirty-one miles of a beach?"

"No way," said Tommy. "Surfing must be the national sport."

"No," said Uncle Richie. "I believe that would be cricket."

When he said that, we all urped. We were, once again, thinking about those grub worms he said Australians liked to eat.

CHAPTER 15

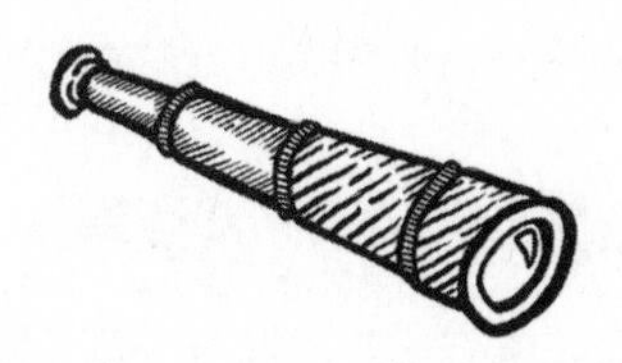

We headed back to our hotel and gathered in Uncle Richie's room around a large map of Australia that we'd purchased in the lobby gift shop.

"Lasseter discovered his reef of gold at the turn of the nineteenth century," said Storm. "But, he, more or less, forgot where it was."

"Guess he didn't have a photographic memory," said Tommy.

Storm nodded. "He tried to go back but he could never retrace his steps or find his gold reef again. Most experts who have studied Lasseter's journals, including Mom and Dad, agree that, if the long-lost treasure actually exists, it would be located somewhere around here." She tapped the map. "Right along the edge of the MacDonnell mountain ranges, putting it west of Alice Springs, a remote town in the deserts of the Northern Territory."

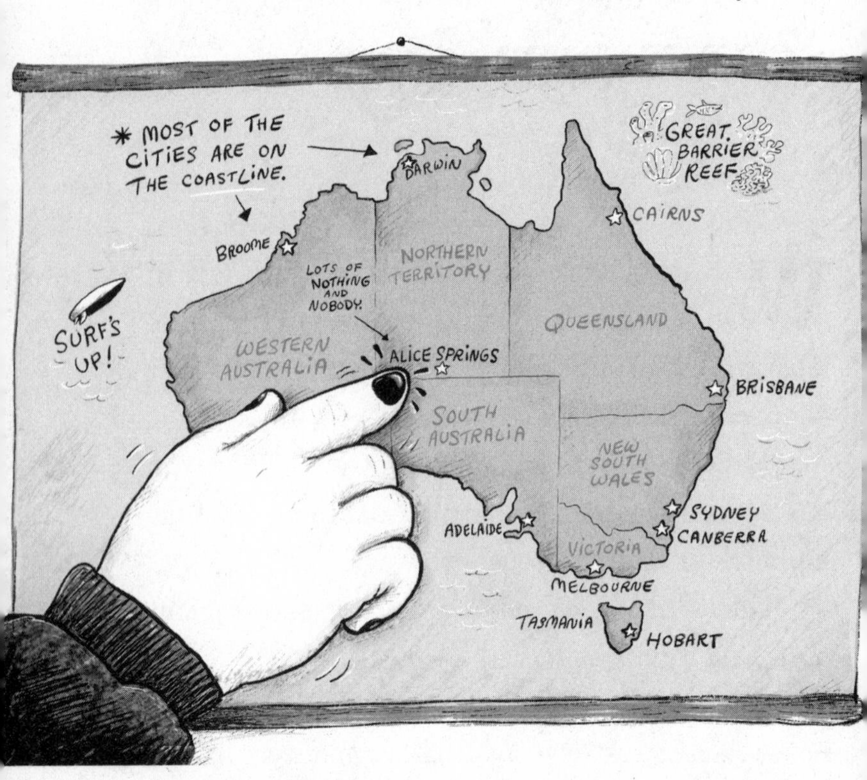

"Alice Springs it is!" said Uncle Richie. "We shall charter a swift aircraft, the swiftest we can find, and fly there tomorrow at first light. Once in the Outback, I feel confident we will quickly overtake Ms. Badger and her associates, Banjo and Croc. We will firmly insist that they immediately turn over the two other opals Detective Superintendent Ruggiere has been hunting down for lo these many years."

"And, if they say no," said Tommy, "then we'll steal the stolen stuff back from them!"

"Agreed," said Uncle Richie. "We need those opals, children. Never forget—the clock is ticking. We only have seven days to save your parents from what, I'm certain, will prove to be a long and severe prison sentence. Thomas?"

"Yes, sir?"

"Make some phone calls. See who will rent us a private jet of some sort."

"Um, okay. But how are we going to pay for it?"

"With this!" He pulled out a shiny black credit card.

"Whoa," said Tommy. "Is that yours?"

"No. It's your mother's. However, in her perpetual pursuit of preparedness, she recently added me as a signatory to the account. This card is available by invitation only and has no spending limit. We can charge whatever we need."

"So, I could buy that Lamborghini I mentioned earlier?"

"Will we need such a vehicle for our current expedition, Thomas? I suspect it might not fare well on the rough and rutted roads of the rugged Australian Outback."

"True. Maybe *after* we grab Badger and the opals, I'll ask Mom about the Lambo."

"That's the spirit, Tommy! Now, if you children will excuse me, I must disappear for the evening."

"Where are you going?" I asked.

"Well, as you might recall, I have many friends, associates, and acquaintances here in Australia, due to my earlier expeditions on the continent. Several of those colleagues will be meeting tonight around a circular table lined with green felt. I thought it might be wise to spend some time with them to see what intelligence I might be able to gather on our nemesis, Charlotte Badger."

"In other words," I said. "you're going to another card game?"

"Yes," said Uncle Richie. "Texas Hold 'Em poker is very popular here, even though we are very far from Texas!"

CHAPTER 16

Uncle Richie put on a snazzy vest with two rows of silver buttons the size of quarters. He also wore what Storm called a silk cravat (it's a swanky bandana).

He looked like a riverboat gambler from an old-fashioned Western movie.

"Wish me luck," he said, giving us a jaunty two-finger salute off his eyebrow. "I hope to come home with actionable intelligence on Ms. Charlotte Badger—as well as a little extra pocket change."

As soon as he was gone, Tommy went to work.

He was on the phone arranging to lease a Falcon 900C business jet.

"I checked out your website. The Falcon comes with a Magnastar satellite phone and an Airshow 400 entertainment system, correct? Cool, man."

There was a pause as the person on the other side of the conversation asked a question.

"With my mother's credit card. It's the black one, dude. You could buy a Lambo with it."

Another pause.

"No, we don't need any pilots. My Uncle Richie has his Australian license. We might need a flight attendant, though."

Storm shot Tommy a dirty look.

"On second thought," Tommy said into the phone, "cancel the flight attendant. We'll pack our own peanuts and soda."

Storm was busy transferring the data from her brain to her laptop, creating a computer-generated map to Lasseter's Gold that would mirror the one locked up in The Room on *The Lost*.

That left Beck and me with nothing to do,

except launch into a Twin Tirade. This was number 2,015, in case you're counting, which we were. In fact, we've actually had several dozen tirades about which number tirade we're on.

"This is such a stupid plan!" said Beck.

"I think it's brilliant!" I shouted back.

"What? We're going to fly to the middle of nowhere, and track down Charlotte Badger, a pirate with a fake name?"

"We're treasure hunters!" I screamed. "Finding stuff, or in this case, people with fake names, is what we do best!"

"And then, once we find them, what are we going to do? Politely ask Charlotte, Banjo, and Croc to turn over the precious jewels they probably stole from someone who stole them twenty years ago!"

"Politeness is a sign of dignity," said Storm, "not subservience. Theodore Roosevelt said that."

"Well, bully for him!" shouted Beck.

"Yeah," I shouted at Storm. "And why are you butting into our argument? This is a Twin Tirade!"

"You're not being very polite, Storm," added Beck. Then she spun back on me. "What are we arguing about?"

"Our stupid plan to snatch the opals off a bunch of pirates," I said.

"Well, it could work," said Tommy. "If we sneak up from behind and conk them in the heads with coconuts."

"Hello?" shouted Storm. "Earth to Tommy. There are no coconuts in the middle of the Australian Outback."

"Not even in the produce section of a high-end grocery store?" said Tommy.

"There aren't many grocery stores in the Outback," said Storm, sounding exasperated. "High-end or otherwise."

"You want to conk them with coconuts?" shrieked Beck. "They probably have pistols!"

"And guns," I added.

"A pistol is a gun!" shouted Beck.

"But is a hot dog a sandwich?" demanded Storm.

"If you put two lasagnas on top of each other,"

shouted Tommy, “is it two lasagnas or just one big one?”

“Who cares?” shouted Beck.

“Me!” said Tommy.

“Is cereal soup?” I wondered.

And then we all argued and screamed about that. For the first time in Kidd family history, a Twin Tirade had turned into a Quadruple Diatribe, a four-way free-for-all. I don’t think our family unit has ever been so un-unified.

Unlike a Twin Tirade, this Quadruple Diatribe didn't fizzle out like the final birthday candle on your cake after you give it one last mighty blow. We kept going for what seemed like hours. We were arguing about everything!

"Toilets swirl backward in Australia!"

"*Barbie* should be a doll, not a barbeque!"

"I don't care what Australians say. Chewy isn't chewing gum! It's a character from *Star Wars*!"

Again, I don't really remember who was screaming what at whom. I think we were all angrier at the situation than one another. Our parents were locked up. They were looking at a long sentence for grand theft jewelry. And the only way for us to save them was to find a bunch of pirates, who had at least a one-day jump on us, and snatch away their opals. And we only had seven days—make that six (because we sure wasted the first day)—to get the job done.

We only stopped screaming at each other when, somehow, we heard a knock on the door.

Things got quiet, fast. We figured a hotel guest

had complained and security had come up to toss us out into the street.

Tommy opened the door.

“Thank you, Thomas. Forgot my key.”

It was Uncle Richie.

“What was all the shouting about?”

“We were, uh, watching Australian TV,” I said because I’m good at making up stories. “They’re way louder than American shows.”

“And their toilets swirl backward,” added Beck.

“Fascinating,” said Uncle Richie. “Were you able to secure us a private jet, Thomas?”

“Yes, sir.”

“Wonderful. We’ll fly south, tomorrow!”

“South?” said Storm. “But Alice Springs is west and north of here.”

“Ah, so it is. But we’re not going to Alice Springs anymore. No, indeed. For I bear new, highly reliable information!”

CHAPTER 17

"So, we're not going out back?" said Tommy.

"It's the Outback, Tommy," said Storm. "Like the steak house."

"Riiiight."

"Change of plans," said Uncle Richie. "One of the fellows sitting around the card table this evening was a gent known as Squinty Eye Joe."

"Does he squint?" I asked.

"Not that I noticed. Then again, the room was rather dark. Anyway, Mr. Joe and I fell into talking. He's best mates with Digger McDaniels, who helped me years ago when I was in the country, searching for a rare Aboriginal artifact.

Digger vouched for me and Squinty Eye Joe told me that he has, as they say, 'done work' for Ms. Charlotte Badger in the past."

"What's Charlotte Badger's real name?" asked Beck.

"The last time she worked with Mr. Joe, she was Catherine Hagerty."

"Because," said Storm, "Catherine Hagerty was a convict sent to Australia by the British who did some pirating with Charlotte Badger."

We all gawked at her.

She shrugged. "I figured I needed to add more Australian pirate trivia to my mental memory chips since I missed that first Charlotte Badger allusion on *The Lost*."

"That's the spirit, Storm," boomed Uncle Richie, clapping her on the back. "But don't be too hard on yourself, dear. A person who never made a mistake never tried anything new!"

"So, what are *we* going to do?" asked Beck.

"Head south," said Tommy. "Right, Uncle Richie?"

"Indeed. For, you see, just yesterday, Charlotte Badger offered Squinty Eye Joe employment on her current expedition. She even showed him the two remaining black opals, offering them as a guarantee of payment should they not find the treasure she was seeking."

"Were they our opals?" I blurted.

"That they were, Bick. Charlotte Badger, it

seems, is a bit of a boaster and braggart. 'These here are called the Pride of Australis and the Black Galaxy,' she told Mr. Joe. 'Rarest missing gemstones in all the land. They're worth three times more than the loot we scored on our last big job.' Mr. Joe also told me that she keeps the two opals secured to her belt in a pair of velvet pouches. One blue. The other green."

"But Squinty Eye Joe turned her down?" I asked.

Uncle Richie nodded. "It was such short notice. Plus, he didn't want to miss his weekly card game. I am also given to understand that Mr. Joe once had a very serious altercation with Ms. Badger's loyal lackey—the fellow known as Banjo. Something to do with knives. Mr. Joe has a rather long and nasty-looking scar that follows the curve of his arched eyebrow. He looks constantly surprised."

"Huh," said Tommy. "I'm still wondering why they call him Squinty Eye. The way you describe him, Bug Eye sounds like a better nickname ..."

"Be that as it may," said Uncle Richie, pulling out a napkin with a map scribbled on it in splotchy blue ink. "We now know where Ms. Badger is headed."

"To dig up Lasseter's Gold, right?" I asked.

"No. That's just what she wants us to think."

"Well," said Beck, "she wins, because we've been thinking it for like five days now."

"Too true," said Uncle Richie. "However, her real quest is the Bonito Treasure!"

"That means 'the good treasure' in Spanish, right?" said Tommy.

Storm shook her head and silently mouthed, *No.*

Uncle Richie waved his napkin map. "This map will guide us to the treasure of another pirate. Benito 'Bloody Sword' Bonito!"

CHAPTER 18

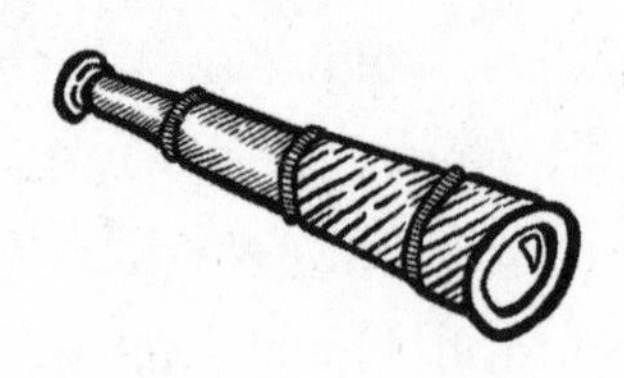

Early the next morning, we packed up what little gear we'd brought with us and hopped into a taxi so we could speed off to Her Majesty's Long Bay Prison to tell Mom and Dad our plans.

On the ride, Storm, who really had memorized a lot of new Australian pirate stuff, gave us a quick, top-line info dump on Benito "Bloody Sword" Bonito.

"Remember all that treasure we found on Cocos Island, before we flew to Peru to find the Lost City of Paititi?"

"The great treasure of Lima!" said Tommy.

"That golden corn cob staff was awesome."

Beck and I glanced at each other warily. We were remembering the hammerhead sharks that swim in the waters surrounding Cocos Island. One of them almost ate us for lunch.

"Well," Storm continued, "Benito 'Bloody Sword' Bonito was a pirate captain terrorizing Spanish galleons up and down the coastline of South America, plundering gold, silver, and jewels and then stashing all that loot up on Cocos."

Beck raised her hand. "What does an island off the coast of Costa Rica have to do with Australia? It's thousands of miles away!"

"Nine thousand, four hundred and seven, to be precise," replied Storm.

"So why do we care about a pirate burying treasure back in the Americas?" I asked. "Even though 'Bloody Sword' is a pretty cool middle name."

"Because, Bickford, on his last attempt to reach the island, Bonito was intercepted and diverted by a British man-o'-war."

“A man-o’-war is an awesome battleship,” said Tommy, turning around from his perch in the front seat, next to the cabbie. “It’s a frigate with cannons and junk!” Then he made several mouth-noise explosions. “Ka-boom! Ka-pow!”

The driver had to wipe spittle off the side of his face.

"Do go on, Storm," said Uncle Richie, who was squeezed into the backseat with me, Beck, and Storm.

"The British ship chased him off course and Bonito headed West…"

"All the way to Australia!" added Uncle Richie. "Where Bloody Sword buried his treasure."

The cabbie looked up into the rearview mirror.

"Any idea where this pirate bloke's treasure might be, mate?" he asked Uncle Richie.

"Sorry, good sir," Uncle Richie answered with a sly grin. "I haven't a clue."

The taxi dropped us off at the prison.

"Visiting another pirate friend?" asked the cabbie as Uncle Richie paid for the ride.

"No," I said. "Just our parents."

As soon as the taxi pulled away, I spun around to face Uncle Richie. "You really *do* know where the treasure's buried, right?"

He tapped the pocket on his safari vest where he'd placed the folded-over map napkin.

"Thanks to Squinty Eye Joe and his mates, I have a pretty good idea."

We all leaned in so he could tell us more.

"Legend has it," he whispered, "Bloody Sword Bonito's treasure is hidden somewhere in the cliffs near the entrance to Port Phillip Bay in Victoria, Australia!"

"Cool!" Tommy whispered back. "But, uh, where's that?"

"Southeast of the city of Melbourne."

"Which is south of Sydney," explained Storm.

"Indeed so. We'll be going just about as south as one can in Australia without ending up in Tasmania."

"Let's go tell Mom and Dad," I said. "And we better make it snappy. We only have five and three quarters days left to retrieve those opals!"

CHAPTER 19

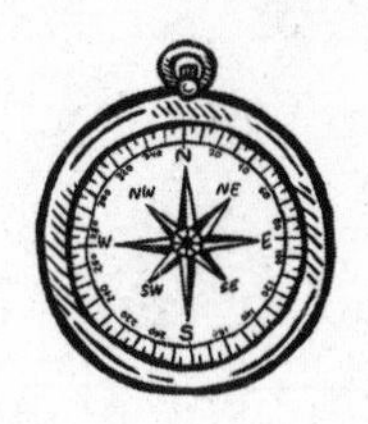

"Ah, yes," said Dad after we were all reunited in the prison's visiting room. "The lost treasure of Benito Bonito. It's been on our list for years."

"Though not at the top," added Mom. "It's not as historically significant or as legendary as Lasseter's Gold."

"But," I said, "that's where Charlotte Badger is going."

"And she has the two opals we need to spring you guys," said Beck.

"There's something else about our research

into Bonito's treasure," said Dad. "But for the life of me, I can't remember it..."

"Don't worry, Dad," said Storm. "Remembering stuff is my job in this family."

"We have a pretty good sense of where Charlotte Badger is headed," said Uncle Richie. "She's such a towering giant of a woman, with extremely easy-to-identify distinguishing characteristics—such as her dreadlocked hair and blazing red bandana—she should be easy to track. We'll just need to ask the right sort of people the right sort of questions. Easy peasy. Nothing to it."

"I don't know, Richie," sighed Dad. "This could be a very dangerous expedition." He stroked his beard thoughtfully.

"Extremely dangerous," echoed Mom, stroking her chin, because she doesn't have a beard to be thoughtful with.

"Danger is my middle name," said Tommy.

"No, it isn't," said Dad.

"It's Aloysius," said Mom. "Thomas Aloysius Kidd."

"Whatever," said Tommy. "We only have, like,

five and three quarters days to grab the jewels off the pirate who framed you guys."

"She keeps them tied to her belt in velvet pouches," said Storm who, remember, remembers everything. "One is blue. The other green."

"I wouldn't be surprised if she had a weapon clipped to that belt as well," said Dad.

"And then there are her crewmates," said Mom. "Benji and Grock."

(Storm did *not* get her photographic memory from Mom.)

"Um, you mean Banjo and Croc," I said, gently correcting her.

"Exactly. Those two scurvy knaves will be armed and dangerous, too."

"So," said Dad, "if you five insist on carrying out this mission ..."

"We do!" we all said together.

"Then," Dad continued, "*we* must insist that you go visit a former colleague of ours. His name is Timbo Tyler."

"He runs an expedition outfitting operation called Camp Billabong," added Mom. "It's not too far from Melbourne. The camp even has its own private landing strip. Timbo knows how to be prepared for any contingency. He'll have all the equipment and gear you'll need. He also knows how to keep a secret."

I raised my hand because, don't forget, Mom is also our main home school teacher.

"Yes, Bick?"

"Did, uh, Mr. Tyler work with you guys, you know—back in the day?"

"You mean when we worked for The Company?" said Dad.

"Yeah."

"Roger that."

I just nodded.

The Company is what Mom and Dad and everybody else who works there calls the CIA. The Central Intelligence Agency.

Did I forget to mention that our parents both used to be spies?

We all hugged and kissed and said our goodbyes. They were speed hugs and kisses, though. That clock was still ticking.

We hailed another cab and headed out to the airfield where Tommy had organized the private jet rental.

"Do you need a map?" asked the lady behind the counter.

"No, thank you," said Uncle Richie. "We're flying, not driving."

"Right. My bad. I used to work for a car rental company."

"Bully for you!" said Uncle Richie.

We all hustled out of the small terminal building and onto the tarmac.

"So, Tommy, how are your flying lessons progressing?" asked Uncle Richie.

"Not bad. I do most of them on a flight simulator game I have on my Xbox."

"Excellent. Perhaps I'll give you the stick once we're airborne."

"Cool."

Giving Tailspin Tommy the stick meant that Uncle Richie was going to let him fly the plane.

I was afraid it might also mean we were all about to die.

Don't forget, we've flown with Tommy in the captain's seat before. Back on our All-American Adventure. I can still remember how the vomit tasted at the back of my mouth.

CHAPTER 20

"Take the stick, Tommy," said Uncle Richie after we'd been airborne for about thirty minutes. "I need to consult this chart. See if I can locate Camp Billabong's landing strip."

"Is that it?" said Tommy, leaning forward to point out the windshield at something. When he did that, his stomach pushed against the control wheel, which actually looked more like padded bicycle handlebars. Pushing the wheel forward sent the plane whining into a nosedive.

Yes, Tommy's lessons hadn't taught him

anything useful. He was still the worst pilot to ever try to fly.

"Pull up on the yoke, Thomas, if you don't mind," said Uncle Richie, kind of calmly, especially considering the fact that the ground was rushing up to greet us.

"Got it," grunted Tommy, pulling on the control wheel with all his might.

He started tapping his toe. He does that sometimes when he's hoisting heavy weights and barbells. In the jet, however, he was tapping his foot on a rudder pedal.

"Oh, my," said Uncle Richie as the plane pulled into a vertical 360-degree tumble. We were hanging out, upside down. I could see the ground. Then the sky. Then the ground again.

Good thing the seat belt sign was still illuminated.

Too bad the cup of soda I'd just poured wasn't wearing one. It splashed and spewed ice cubes down at the ceiling.

"Y-y-ou w-w-want t-t-to t-t-take o-o-over,

U-U-Uncle R-R-Richie?" stammered Tommy as the G-forces of the climbs and dives made his cheeks wobble and flop.

"N-n-no n-n-need," shouted Uncle Richie. "You've got this, Thomas."

"Activating air brakes!" Tommy cried.

"I wouldn't—"

Tommy yanked a lever.

"—do that," said Uncle Richie as we twirled into a series of sideways rolls. "Air brakes will increase the speed of the roll."

It felt like we were inside a washing machine during the spin cycle. Somewhere my underpants might need to be if we ever landed.

"Fascinating, Thomas," said Uncle Richie, as we climbed up into a steep arc and spun around to, once again, aim for the ground. "You just executed a perfect double hammerhead maneuver!"

"Really?"

"You're going to be a great pilot, Tommy!"

"And the rest of us are all gonna be dead!" Beck shouted from the cabin, where *her* soda can was glued sideways to the window.

TOMMY MIGHT FLY WITH THE BLUE ANGELS SOMEDAY.
OR WE MIGHT CRASH AND TURN INTO REAL ANGELS TODAY.

"There it is!" shouted Uncle Richie. "Up ahead on the right. The left. Okay, the right again. It's the Camp Billabong landing strip. Well done, Thomas! This location is so remote, I don't think we could've found it if you hadn't initiated so many unorthodox barrel rolls, loop-de-loops, tail slides, inverted spins, and whatever those other moves were that you improvised. You've done your job, lad, and done it well. I'll line us up for landing."

I almost relaxed.

But then I saw the kangaroo herd stampeding across the dirt and gravel runway.

After that, all anybody could see was a cloud of reddish dust.

"Hang on, children," boomed Uncle Richie. "I think I'm lined up for the runway. Or it could be a clump of coolabah trees. Either way, I suspect it's going to be a bumpy landing."

Ya think? I wanted to say.

But I didn't.

I was too busy saying my prayers.

CHAPTER 21

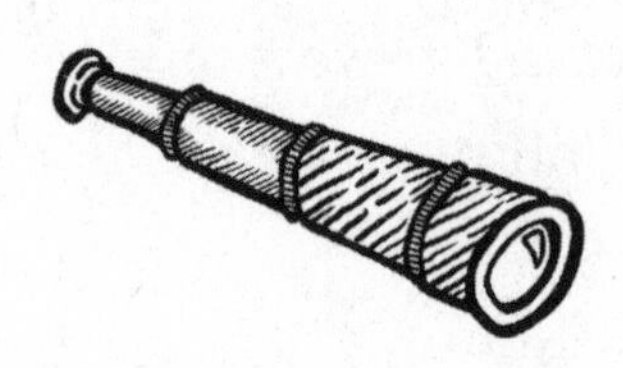

Beck and I wobbled out of the plane, fell to our knees, and kissed the ground because we were so happy to be alive.

I said a silent prayer: *"Never, ever let Tommy pilot a plane again. Please."*

Storm came over with a major *yuck* look on her face.

"Um, you guys do realize that some of those kangaroos stampeding across the runway probably pooped. Just saying."

"Well done, Thomas," said Uncle Richie, as he and Tommy came marching across the tarmac.

"You'll have your license in no time!"

"Thanks, Uncle Richie. I like aeronautics even better than regular nautics. You know, the kind on water."

"Well, you definitely have a knack for it," Uncle Richie told him.

Beck and I would beg to disagree. Unless by "knack" Uncle Richie meant the talent and ability to hurl passengers face-first into their barf bags.

"That must be the camp's HQ," said Uncle Richie, pointing to a small building with a slanted tin roof and a dusty, railed-in porch. Half a dozen kangaroos were hanging out in the scrubby lawn in front of the building. And, yes, one was pooping.

Suddenly, two kids, a boy and girl who looked to be about the same age as Beck and me, came running around the side of the cabin. They were flinging boomerangs at each other. The bad news was, when the boomerangs missed their targets because the kids both ducked, the whirling, blunt blades returned to their throwers and banged them in their bellies.

"Oof!" cried the girl when the boomerang walloped her in the gut. "You're a dingaling."

"So," shouted the boy, taking hold of the boomerang and taking aim at the girl. "You're a drongo and a droob!"

"At least I'm not a dingaling."

"Drongo!"

"Ah, I wouldn't use you for shark bait!"

"Because you're lower than a snake's belly!"

And then they tore off into the trees, flinging their boomerangs at each other again.

"Shall we hurry inside before the boomerang bombardment returns?" suggested Uncle Richie.

"Good idea," said Tommy.

We all scurried past the kangaroos, up the three plank steps, and onto the covered porch.

"G'day, mates! 'Ow yer goin'?" A man in a black cowboy hat creaked open the rattly screen door and strode out onto the porch. His hat was circled by a band of sharp teeth and had an emu feather sticking out of it. He wore an open leather vest, more teeth on a necklace, and lots of bronzed muscles. "You must be the Kidds."

"Indeed, they are," said Uncle Richie. "And I am their great uncle Richie."

"Cooee, digger. Reckon, you have a mighty big impression of yourself, eh?"

"Actually," said Storm, "he is technically correct. Richie 'Poppie' Luccio is our great uncle because he is our mother's uncle."

"Then I'll be a monkey's uncle, little sheila."

"Um, her name is Storm," said Tommy.

"Sheila is what Australians sometimes call females," explained Storm.

"Even though it's not your name? Weird."

The man boomed a big laugh.

"Welcome to Oz, cobbers. The wonder down under. Where everything is a wee bit upside down!"

CHAPTER 22

"Allow me to introduce myself, bugalugs," said the man. "I'm Timbo Tyler. Fair dinkum

friend and former colleague of your parents.

"I knew your old crackers back in the day when we were all tin ears."

"Does that mean you were a spy?" I asked.

"Too right."

"Um, does that mean, 'yes'?"

"Crikey. Are you working on a slang dictionary, boyo?"

"Sort of."

"Then, yes," said Timbo Tyler. "Let's just say I was an associate of your parents back in our dark and clandestine days."

Beck turned to me. "He was a spy."

"I'm also a renowned crocodile wrestler," said Mr. Tyler.

"Get out!" said Tommy, sounding impressed.

"How do you think I made this necklace and my hat band?"

He pointed to the string of teeth dangling across his chest.

"Arts and crafts at summer camp?" said Storm drily.

"Weren't no summer camp where I snagged

these souvenirs, luv. Not to boast, but the crocodile got the worst of it. When we were done with our barney, he had to go straight to the dentist."

Uncle Richie tossed back his head and laughed. "Good one, Mr. Tyler! Jolly good."

"Are those boomerangs?" asked Storm pointing to a bucket filled with angled wood wedges, all of them decorated with primitive paintings.

"That they are. Help yourself to one, if you fancy."

Storm rustled through the bucket and pulled out a boomerang with all sorts of colorful art painted on its sides. She tested its heft in her hand and did a few little wrist flicks. She must've liked the way it felt because she smiled, something Storm doesn't do all that often.

"Thanks," she said.

"No worries," said Timbo Tyler. "Say, do any of you folks know what you call a boomerang that won't come back?"

"Yeah," said Beck. "A stick."

"Good on ya, Rebecca," said Tyler, with a hearty laugh.

"How'd you know my name?"

"Just something we spies are good at. Also, your parents were allowed one phone call this morning at the prison. They called me. Said you lot would be flying down. Needed to get outfitted for an expedition."

"Indeed, we do," said Uncle Richie. "We need the full package, Timbo. A vehicle. Provisions. Camping gear."

"Weapons," said Tommy.

Uncle Richie shook his head. "I don't think guns will be necessary, Thomas."

"Seriously?" I said. "We're going up against pirates! They'll have guns plus knives, swords, and cutlasses."

"A cutlass *is* a sword," said Storm.

"See?" I said to Uncle Richie. "They're so heavily armed, they have two different kinds of swords. And what do we have?"

"Nothing!" said Beck, finishing my thought. It's

a twin thing. "We have zip, zilch, nada, bubkes."

"Tut, tut," said Uncle Richie. "We will have our cunning, our wits, and, of course, our courage. We won't need guns."

"How about a knife?" said Tommy.

"Oh, I can let you have this little toothpicker," said Timbo Tyler, pulling out a blade that had to be at least a foot and a half long.

"In fact, I can give you everything you need," Mr. Tyler told us. "For free."

"Free?" I said. "That's awesome!"

"Too right. I'll give you whatever you require for your trek. Of course, there is one minor proviso. One teeny, tiny favor I'll ask in return."

"Seems fair," said Uncle Richie.

"What is it?" said Beck, who handles a lot of our negotiations for supplies when we're on *The Lost*.

"Just that you take my darling li'l niece and nephew with you. They're twins. Terry and Tabitha. They're from Tasmania. In fact, their mum and dad call them the Tasmanian Terrors."

CHAPTER 23

You know, I used to think Tommy, Storm, Beck, and I were the energetic ones, always ready for a wild rumpus.

Then we met Terry and Tabitha Tyler.

They were the kids we'd seen earlier—chasing each other around Timbo Tyler's lodge, bopping themselves with boomerangs. They had a kind of crazed look in their eyes. They also had a band of snarling tattoos ringing their arms—and they were only twelve years old.

You know those Twin Tirades Beck and I sometimes throw?

We were amateurs compared to Terry and Tabitha.

They tumbled around the corner of the house, chasing after a kangaroo.

Their uncle stuck two fingers into his lips and whistled the kind of whistle people use to call home their dogs, if their dogs are in the next county.

"Terry? Tabitha? Get over here, you two. I want you to meet your new traveling mates."

The two rowdy siblings let the kangaroo run away and kind of scuffled over.

"Traveling?" said Terry, the boy, spitting on the ground. "We like it here."

"Speak for yourself," said Tabitha.

"I just did!"

"I thought I smelled something. Your breath is like an emu fart."

"Well yours is a blight on my bugle," said Terry, tapping his nose. When he did, a dried booger fell out.

OH, YOU'RE AS FUNNY AS A FART ON AN ELEVATOR!
YOU HAVE A FACE LIKE A DROPPED PIE!
AH, DON'T GO OFF LIKE A FROG IN A SOCK.
YOU'RE NOTHING BUT A LAZY BLUDGER!
WOW. THESE GUYS ARE GOOD.

The Tasmanian Terrors' Tirade was such a scorcher, it even woke up the super mellow koala hanging out in a nearby eucalyptus tree.

"Pack your things, Terry and Tabitha," said their uncle. "You'll be leaving straight away."

"Where's my toothbrush?" said Terry as he and Tabitha pushed and elbowed each other up the steps, trying to be the first into the house.

"In the bathroom, of course," said Tabitha. "I used it to scrub the toilet."

"May your chooks turn into emus," said Terry, "and kick down your dunny door."

They shoved their way inside. We all turned to Storm.

"That one was something about chickens turning into angry birds the size of ostriches with very strong legs that would kick open the entryway to an outhouse," she explained.

"They have a bit of an independent streak, I'll grant you that," said their Uncle Timbo with a sly grin. "Pair of fair dinkum scrubbers."

"Family meeting?" I said, gesturing with my

head that we should all step away from the porch so we could speak in private.

"Will you give us a minute?" Uncle Richie said to Mr. Tyler.

"Have at it!"

We bustled away from the Camp Billabong building in a bunch.

"Those two Tasmanian Terrors are going to slow us down!" I whispered when we were huddled together, maybe fifteen feet from the porch.

"They're horrible," said Beck.

"Must be a twin thing," Storm muttered to Tommy.

"Chya."

"But we need equipment," said Uncle Richie. "Vehicles. Supplies. We're running out of time. And Ms. Badger's lead on us increases every minute we delay. Unfortunately, taking along an extra pair of twins on this expedition is the price we must pay."

"Can't we just use Mom's credit card?" I asked.

"He won't take it," said Storm. "I have a feeling

being temporarily free of his niece and nephew is worth more to Mr. Tyler than all the money in the world."

"Oh, by the way!" Mr. Tyler shouted from the porch through cupped hands. "I forgot to mention something."

"What?" Tommy shouted back.

"I know exactly where Ms. Badger is and where she's headed. Take the Tasmanian twins off my hands, and I'll gladly share that information with you."

CHAPTER 24

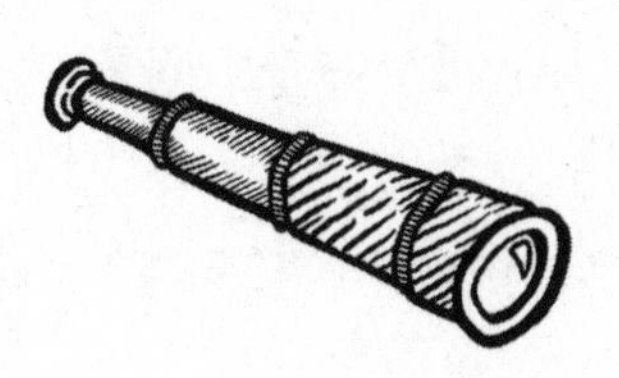

Turns out, Timbo Tyler's Camp Billabong was the only expert expedition outfitter in the region.

Charlotte Badger had stopped by to get her treasure-hunting equipment there, less than twenty-four hours ago!

Because she and Mr. Tyler knew each other from "back in the day."

"In my work for the Australian Secret Intelligence Service," he told us, "I met many nefarious and unsavory characters. Let's just say I've met the dodgy Ms. Badger before."

"Do you know her real name?" asked Tommy.

"That I do, lad. It's Trouble with a capital T."

"Seriously?"

"I believe Mr. Tyler is making a point," said Uncle Richie.

"Oh. Okay. You grown-ups do that a lot, don't you?"

"We try," said Mr. Tyler. "Now then, since you have agreed to take my charming niece and nephew along with you on your adventure ..."

I turned to Uncle Richie. "We have?"

He nodded. It was a done deal. Because our week to retrieve the opals was disappearing faster than an open bag of potato chips at a picnic.

"Since you will be taking Terry and Tabitha along for the ride, I should let you know that Ms. Badger has the jump on you lot. She stopped by yesterday. Told me she was interested in doing a little sightseeing with her mates."

"How many pirates were traveling with her?" I asked.

THIS BOBBY DAZZLER OF A BEAUT WAS ONLY DRIVEN ON SUNDAYS BY A LITTLE OLD LADY WHO LIKED TO WRESTLE WALLABIES. COMES STANDARD WITH THE ROO BAR UP FRONT.
WE'LL TAKE IT, MATE.

"Two. I believe their names were Banjo and Croc."

"Ah, excellent," said Uncle Richie. "She never did find the additional crew member she'd been searching for in Sydney. That means she wasted time searching for talent and that she won't be working this treasure hunt as swiftly as she had hoped. I like our chances, children. I like them a lot."

Beck and I looked at each other. Both of us would've liked our chances better if we had Tasers. Or even a tranquilizer gun.

"Did she have two velvet pouches tied to her belt?" asked Storm. "One blue, the other green."

"She had the pouches," said Mr. Tyler. "But I don't recall the colors."

"That's okay," said Storm. "I do."

"That means she still has the two opals we need!" said Tommy. "Good question, Storm!"

"Thanks."

"Anyway," said Mr. Tyler, "I fixed up Charlotte Badger and her ratty team with a four-wheel-drive Aussie Troopie vehicle, camping gear, excavating equipment, and a box of dynamite."

"Dynamite?" said Beck.

Mr. Tyler just nodded.

"I also gave her a piece of equipment she didn't ask for and I'll wager she doesn't even know she has."

"What is it?" asked Beck.

"A GPS tracking device. Secretly secured to the undercarriage. Here you go."

He handed Uncle Richie what looked like a tracking device.

"That blinking red dot? That's your opal thief."

Uncle Richie took the tracker and shook Mr. Tyler's hand. "We have a deal, Timbo. But, we'll need *two* vehicles. I'll drive one. Tommy, here, the other. After all, there are seven of us now."

Yep.

Tabitha and Terry were coming with us.

I figured they could be our dynamite.

CHAPTER 25

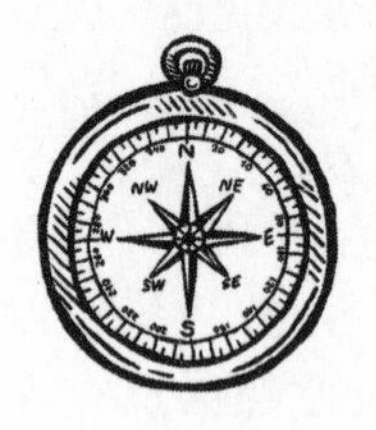

When Uncle Richie and Tommy walked over to the garage with Mr. Tyler to check out a few vehicles, Storm immediately jumped on her laptop, watched a few YouTube videos, and, in a flash, became an expert boomerang flinger.

"I'm throwing right-handed with a cradle grip which means my left arm is my dingle," she told us. "Once I analyze wind direction and velocity, my throw will be no more than forty-five degrees from vertical, forty to sixty degrees off the wind, and I won't sidearm it or the boomerang will climb too high and crash. Of course, spin will be key. Just like tossing a football!"

Beck and I just stood there gawking as she flicked the sleek, angle-armed wing of wood exactly like she said she would.

"You know," said Storm, as she waited for her twirling boomerang to complete its circuit around the property and come back to her, "a boomerang is actually a type of throwing star that originated in Australia as a hunting weapon used by its Aboriginal people."

"Awesome," I said. "It's like going hunting with a Labrador retriever that brings stuff back to you."

"The boomerang doesn't retrieve stuff, Bick. It just knocks it down." Storm reached up and made a two-handed grab of her returning boomerang. "The boomerang is also a rare example of a non-ballistic missile."

"Huh?" Beck and I said together.

"It doesn't go up and down in an arc like a spear or arrow or a cannonball. The boomerang flies parallel to the ground and, if it's rotating fast enough, can fight gravity."

"It would also hurt if it hit you, right?" I asked.

"Definitely," said Storm. "You could even break someone's leg. They're also excellent at clipping things—like fruit or nuts off branches in a high tree."

"You guys?" I said. "We should grab a few more of these boomerangs. They're weapons! And we might need weapons when we go up against those pirates."

The three of us hurried back to the porch where we each pulled a heavy wooden wing out of the bucket. They were all painted with what Storm called "traditional Aboriginal designs."

"What exactly does Aboriginal mean?" I asked.

"The people who inhabited this land before the first European settlers showed up," explained Storm. "Aboriginal peoples are the first peoples of mainland Australia and many of its islands, such as Tasmania."

That's when we heard a really weird sound.

A rolling drone—like a foghorn from outer space.

The noise warbled on and on.

I wondered, *"Did some kind of UFO just park on that Camp Billabong landing strip?"*

CHAPTER 26

"If I'm not mistaken," said Storm, "that music is being made by an indigenous wind instrument known as a didgeridoo!"

"Music?" said Beck, covering her ears.

"Storm uses the term loosely," I said. "It sounds more like a really long elephant fart."

"Or a dump truck stuck in a tunnel with a broken air horn," said Beck.

Storm ignored us and shoved open the screen door. We followed her into the Camp Billabong Lodge.

Terry and Tabitha, the Tasmanian Terrors, were sitting on squat stools, blowing into long wooden tubes decorated with more of that traditional Aboriginal Australian art. The twins were breathing in through their noses and blowing out through their mouths to keep each long tube vibrating one very deep and rumbly note. They were also rattling all the glass in the building. And some of the furniture. I could hear jars jiggling inside a refrigerator.

"Those carvings along the sides of the didgeridoos are fascinating," said Storm, scanning a stack of the wooden tubes propped up in a corner. She dug deep into the pile to study one didgeridoo even more closely.

"Fascinating!" she said again.

"I just wish the music was fascinating, too," said Beck.

"It is!" said Storm. "Moody. Mysterious. Marvelous!"

Tabitha and Terry kept the buzzing hum going for five full minutes, eyeballing each other the

whole time. It was like they were having a staring contest, except, instead of blinking, they were trying to see who could keep their drone going the longest without breaking for a breath.

Finally, Terry threw in the towel. He pulled the tube away from his face, gasped down some air, and shouted, "I want a snack!"

Tabitha stopped blowing, too. "Ha! I won."

"No, you didn't. I'm just calling a snack break."

"You're a dipstick, Terry!" screamed Tabitha. "You can't call a snack break in the middle of a didgeridoo duel!"

"Really? Because I just did."

"And I just creamed you!"

"Did not!"

"Did, too!"

"Not!"

"Too!"

Storm looked at Beck and me. "Sound familiar?"

"No," I said. "We don't have Australian accents."

Fortunately, that's when Timbo Tyler strode into the room. Uncle Richie and Tommy were right behind him. Mr. Tyler did that loud, two-finger whistle thing he does so well.

TWEEEEEET!

Terry and Tabitha froze.

"Finish packing your kit, kids," said Mr. Tyler.

"You two are taking off for a few days. I'll miss you, for sure. But, well, this is a once in a lifetime opportunity! A real bobby dazzler!"

"You're going on a treasure hunt with us!" boomed Uncle Richie.

"Cool," said Terry.

"Lame," said Tabitha.

"Cool!"

"Lame!"

Yep.

One thing was clear: Terry and Tabitha's Twin Tirades never, *ever* ended.

CHAPTER 27

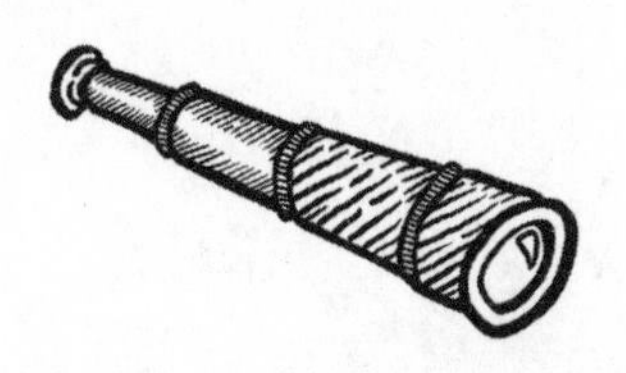

We took off from Camp Billabong in a pair of four-wheel-drive, all-terrain vehicles.

Beck, Storm, and I bumped along in the lead vehicle with Uncle Richie. The Tasmanian Terrors were riding with Tommy. He had personally strapped them into their seat belts in the back. He also cranked up the road trip tunes. Loud.

We were following the tracking device that Mr. Tyler had planted under the chassis of Charlotte Badger's Aussie Troopie vehicle. She was heading to Port Phillip.

If that's where she and the opals were, that's where we needed to be.

ARE WE THERE YET?
ARE WE THERE YET?!
ARE WE THERE YET?
ARE WE THERE YET?
ARE WE THERE YET?

"We should probably call Mom and Dad," suggested Beck. "Let them know we are on the move!"

"And," I added, "that we're getting closer to the treasure we need to set them free."

"Make the call, Storm!" said Uncle Richie.

Storm was sitting up front, riding shotgun. She jabbed a number into the secure satellite phone Timbo Tyler had lent us. Mr. Tyler had also given us the unlisted phone number (that none of us knew) to reach Mom and Dad—if one of them was still wearing their top-secret spy watch from "back in the day."

"Hello?" whispered Dad. Of course. His dive watch was also a spy watch!

"Hey! Hi! Hello!" we all whispered back, because Storm had us on speakerphone.

"How are you holding up, Thomas?" asked Uncle Richie.

"They're treating us well."

"Except for the Vegemite on toast for breakfast," said Mom. "That could be considered torture."

"On a positive note, they allowed me to keep my watch," said Dad.

"They thought it might make us more miserable," added Mom. "After all, we are in here serving 'time.'"

"Hang in there, Sue," said Uncle Richie. "And know that we have rendezvoused with Timbo Tyler. We are well equipped and provisioned and heading south. As luck would have it, your enterprising friend, that master of espionage, Mr. Timbo Tyler, was able to plant a tracking device on Ms. Badger's vehicle. It's leading us straight to her location."

"Excellent," said Dad.

"So far so good," said Uncle Richie, "but it seems she has parked her vehicle. Her tracking beacon has remained frozen for quite some time now."

"She's probably on foot," said Mom. "Searching for Bonito's treasure up in the cliffs and caves near the bay. Storm?"

"Yes, Mom?"

"Now would be a good time for you to remember the tale of Stingaree Jack."

"It's what I couldn't remember when you visited us in the jail!" added Dad. "We used to read it to you when you were a baby. It was a picture book. The boy with the tattoo map on his arm?"

Storm's tilted her head sideways like a puppy that thinks it just heard someone call its name. Her eyes sort of glazed over. I half expected them to turn into a pair of spinning rainbow swirls, like a computer has when it's downloading information.

"Of course!" said Storm. "Stingaree Jack. Got it!"

"Good," whispered Dad. "We need to terminate this call. A guard is coming. I don't want him to see me talking to my wristwatch! Good luck! Happy treasure hunting. Follow the tattoo map, Storm! That's what Charlotte Badger is undoubtedly doing."

The call cut out.

"And who, pray tell, is this Stingaree Jack fellow?" Uncle Richie asked Storm.

"And what's this about a map?" I added.

"Stingaree Jack was the hero of a picture book that, if I remember correctly, which, of course, I always do, Mom and Dad wrote and illustrated themselves. It was all about a cabin boy named Stingaree Jack who escaped from Benito 'Bloody Sword' Bonito's ship with a treasure map tattooed on his arm!"

"A map that Mom and Dad drew from the research they'd done!" shouted Beck.

Storm nodded. "Yes. They were always incorporating actual treasure hunting skills and research into our bedtime stories."

"Do you remember the map?" I asked.

"Now I do," said Storm.

"Can you draw it?" asked Beck.

"Well, duh," she said as she started drawing a map on the side of a brown paper lunch sack. "What's the point of having a photographic memory if you can't make a few photocopies from time to time?"

CHAPTER 28

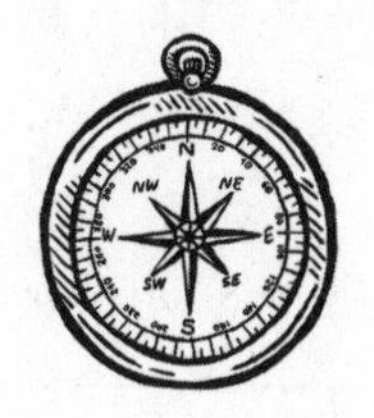

"You guys?" I said, as Storm completed drawing her very detailed map. "If we really know where Bloody Sword Bonito's treasure is buried . . ."

"We do," said Storm. "And it's not buried; it's sealed in a cave."

"Even better," I said. "We forgot to pack shovels."

Storm ran her finger along the dotted line of her map. "There is a rock at the first falls with a horse head carved into it. That horse's nose is pointing to a big rock with a dagger carved into it. The dagger points to a rock with an arrow that points to a second waterfall. The treasure cave is hidden behind the second waterfall."

"All that was tattooed on some kid's arm?" said Beck.

"Some of the best tattoo artists in the world are scattered across the islands of the South Pacific," said Uncle Richie. "Have been for centuries. I imagine Bloody Sword sealed the entrance to his treasure cave with dynamite."

Storm nodded. "That would explain this image near the entrance. I thought it was a firecracker. There's also a skull-and-crossbones slashed into the boulders blocking the entrance—an X marking the spot where the treasure is hidden."

"Ms. Badger is undoubtedly following the same map," said Uncle Richie.

"Yeah!" I said. "That's why she packed the dynamite. To blast the door open again!"

"Indeed," said Uncle Richie. "And, legend has it, inside that sealed cavern, Captain Bloody Sword Bonito stashed four life-size golden figures, each one studded with jewels."

"Wow," I said. "No wonder Bonito's lost treasure has been on Mom and Dad's list for such a long time..."

“But not near the top,” said Beck.

“But, still. It was on the list. Plus, they were doing research on it since before we were even born. They even wrote a picture book about it. That means we should go get it!”

“What?” said Beck.

“If we’re going up to the cave behind the waterfall anyhow, we might as well grab a few golden mannequins studded with jewels while we’re there! Mom and Dad will be so proud.”

“Remember the task at hand, Bickford,” said Uncle Richie.

“Well, who says we can’t do both?” I wondered out loud. “Retrieve the opals *and* grab Bonito’s treasure!”

“Um, Charlotte Badger would probably say that,” said Storm.

“It’s a dumb idea, Bick,” said Beck.

“You mean a genius idea!” I shot back.

“Okay, if by genius you mean idiotic!”

Yes, we were erupting into a mini Twin Tirade, right there in the backseat. It happens sometimes on road trips. Especially since we couldn’t really play license plate bingo. There weren’t any other cars on the dusty dirt road, except Tommy, who was right behind us.

"We only have five days left, Bickford!" shouted Beck.

"So what, Rebecca? We only need one day to finish the job!"

"The pirates have weapons!"

"We have boomerangs. And Storm."

"We didn't bring any dynamite!"

"So we'll use theirs."

"Oh, great. That's something else we need to grab off a group of gnarly scallywags. Opals, dynamite, and jewel-encrusted statues!"

"I want all that gold and jewelry, Beck!"

"And I want a new twin brother."

"Seriously?"

"No way. One twin brother is enough."

"If you had two, we'd be triplets."

"That'd be weird."

"Totally."

Yes, our tirade was in the cooldown stage.

"Okay," I said, "let's just go for the opals. But if Charlotte Badger wants to give us the dynamite and the golden statues, we'll take them."

"Deal."

We shook on it.

"Uh-oh," said Uncle Richie, glancing up into the rearview mirror. "Looks like trouble."

"No trouble back here," I said. "We're all done."

"Totally," added Beck. "We're cool."

"Bully for you two," said Uncle Richie, slamming on the brakes. "Thomas, on the other hand, isn't quite so fortunate. It seems his vehicle has rolled over and landed, tires-up, in a swampy bog."

CHAPTER 29

The four of us tumbled out of the lead vehicle and ran back to make sure Tommy, Terry, and Tabitha were okay.

The three of them, looking slightly dazed, were wading through the murky water. It was up to Tommy's thighs and the Tasmanian twins' chests.

"Are any of you injured, Thomas?" cried Uncle Richie when we reached the edge of the shallow swamp.

"I'm okay," said Tommy. "But I'm not sure about Tabitha and Terry. They haven't screamed at each other once since we flipped over."

"Why'd you wreck?" I asked.

"Because these two were bored sitting in the backseat. They decided to climb up front with me. Then Terry wanted to drive, so he jumped into my lap and took the wheel. Then Tabitha decided *she* wanted to drive, too. So, she jumped into Terry's lap and wrestled the wheel away from him. There was a lot of wheel twisting, back and forth. That's, more or less, when we wiped out."

"It's all Terry's fault!" shouted Tabitha. "He's a clumsy, cack-handed boofhead!"

"Am not," screamed Terry. "Tabitha's just dilly. If brains were dynamite, she couldn't blow off her hat!"

"Um, you guys?" said Storm.

No one paid attention to her. Tommy was covering his ears and the Tasmanian Terrors were still screaming at each other.

"You have a face like a sucked mango!" hollered Tabitha.

"Then so do you!" Terry shot back. "We're twins, remember?"

Storm tried again. "You guys?"

Tabitha swatted at the air. "Onya bike, Terry. Tell your story walkin'!"

"Don't have a bike, Tabitha. Can't walk. Water's too deep."

"And that log just moved!" Storm shouted.

Only it wasn't a log.

It was a crocodile.

A giant crocodile! The thing had to be at least ten feet long. It was lurking at the edge of the little lagoon.

Until it wasn't.

Jaws open, it lunged into the water, gunning for Tommy, Tabitha, and Terry.

"Go for the eyes," shouted Storm, who must've memorized a survivalist book about how to fight off a crocodile. "Poke it in the eyeballs! It's the only way to fend off an attack!"

"Listen to your sister, Thomas!" shouted Uncle Richie. "Poke that blasted beast in the eyeballs!"

"Can't poke," said Tommy, scooping up Terry and Tabitha. He cradled them under his arms. "My hands are busy." He dragged his legs through the water and, moving in slow motion, tried to haul the Tasmanian twins to safety.

But the croc was fast. Faster than Tommy, especially when he's carrying two kicking and screaming kids. The crocodile also had jaws (Storm told us later) that could clamp down with the power of thirteen tons per square inch. Its skin was so thick, you couldn't pierce it. Its head was a solid mass of hard bone.

That's when Storm pulled out the boomerang she had tucked into her belt and sent it whirling.

She, of course, was aiming for the eyeballs.

The creature snapped open its jaws. It was about to take a big bite of Tommy's butt when, *BAM!*

Storm's boomerang bopped it in the right eyeball.

It froze.

Just long enough for Tommy to scamper out of the water with the Tasmanian Terrors.

They weren't even hurt.

We could tell.

Because they started screaming at each other again.

CHAPTER 30

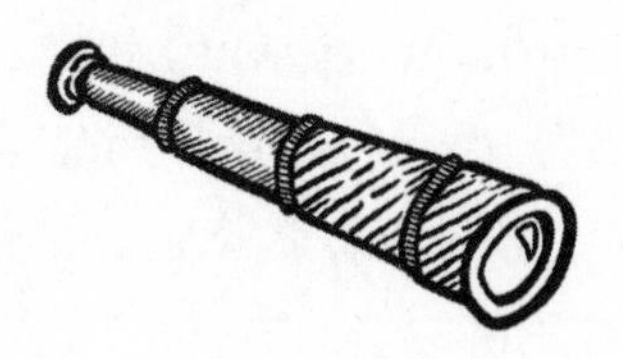

While Terry and Tabitha screeched themselves blue in the background, Uncle Richie called Timbo Tyler's secret number on the spy phone.

"G'day?" Tyler said when he answered *his* watch.

"Timbo? Richie Luccio here. Sad to say, we're in a bit of a sticky wicket. One of the vehicles you lent us is stuck in a swamp. Upside down. I can send you the GPS coordinates ..."

"No need, mate," we heard Mr. Tyler say through the phone. "I popped a tracker on your vehicles, too. Standard practice ’round here. How are Terry and Tabitha?”

Uncle Richie’s gaze drifted off to where the Tasmanian twins were making mud pies and slapping them in each other’s faces.

“Smashing. Timbo? I wonder if I might ask another favor?”

“Name it, mate.”

“Well, once we acquire the opals from Ms. Badger, I suspect we might need to beat a hasty retreat. Something that might prove difficult with just one Land Rover and seven people.”

“Too right. Reckon it’ll be a regular bush bash, you lot trying to outrun the pirates.”

“You wouldn’t have access to, oh, let’s say, a helicopter?”

“An egg beater? No worries, mate. When you need the whirlybird, just give me another jingle on the blower.”

“The, uh, phone?”

“Right. That’s what I said. The blower.”

“Bully. Again, our gratitude.”

“Just keep my niece and nephew safe and

secure, and I'll be happy as a box full of birds."

"Actually," said Storm, "the birds wouldn't be very happy if they were trapped in a box..."

Uncle Richie put a finger to his lips and winked at Storm. He didn't think this was the time for an Australian slang debate.

And so, with our emergency extradition plan in place (the helicopter, unless Timbo Tyler was really going to send us an egg beater), we crammed into our one remaining vehicle.

"You and Beck need to ride up on the luggage rack," said Tommy, after Uncle Richie, Storm, Terry, and Tabitha had squeezed into the Land Rover and taken up every available inch.

"What?" Beck and I said together. It was less of a twin thing; more of a blowflies-in-our-teeth thing.

"We don't have much farther to travel," said Uncle Richie. "According to our tracker, Ms. Badger is parked less than a mile away!"

And so we rode that mile up on the roof of a bouncing Rover. I still have the luggage-rack marks on my hands and knees to prove it.

Finally, Tommy brought the vehicle to a stop—right behind an abandoned Aussie Troopie parked on the shoulder of the road. There was a sign welcoming us to Point Nepean National Park. We could see Port Phillip Bay. It looked like a perfect place to park a pirate ship.

"That's Charlotte Badger's vehicle!" said Tommy as he bounded out.

"But where's Charlotte Badger?" said Storm, as she came stumbling out of the cramped back-seat.

"Therein lies our problem," said Uncle Richie, thoughtfully stroking his chin, the way Mom and Dad do when they don't have an answer. "Which way did she go?"

"That way," said Terry, pointing to a clump of trees.

"And she's with two men," added Tabitha. "One of them is carrying something heavy."

"Probably a box of dynamite," said Terry.

"We better hurry," said Tabitha.

Terry nodded. "They left their vehicle two, maybe three hours ago."

Uncle Richie, Storm, Beck, Tommy, and I all had our jaws hanging open.

"Don't just stand there with your jaws hanging open!" said Tabitha. "You heard what Terry said. If you want to catch your pirates, we need to do it, now!"

CHAPTER 31

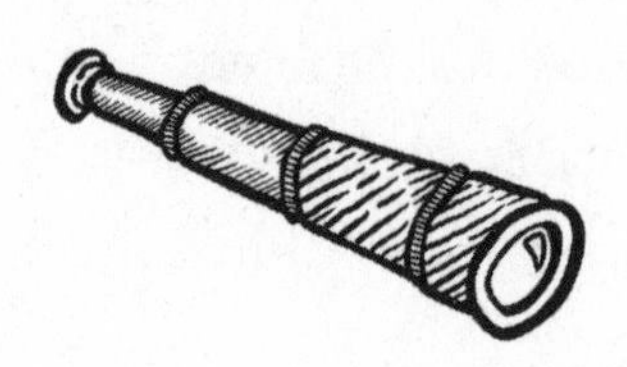

We all trooped behind Terry and Tabitha. They led us through a tangle of scrubby underbrush and up onto the limestone cliffs ringing the southern shore of Port Phillip Bay.

"So, uh, how do you guys know we're heading the right way?" I asked.

"Because our mother's people were here long before any of you European types," snarled Terry.

"She taught us how to read the land," said Tabitha, sounding irritated. "How to track anything. Animal, human—even birds."

"Ah," said Uncle Richie, "I take it your mother is of Aboriginal descent?"

"She's a Palawa!" snapped Tabitha.

"That's the proper name for an Aboriginal Tasmanian," explained Storm.

"Well, duh, you boofhead," said Terry. "Tabitha just told you that."

Then the two of them slapped each other a high five.

"Aboriginal trackers are celebrated throughout Australian history," said Storm, ready to give us another information dump. "In 1864, they were able to locate the three missing Duff children, who had been lost for three days, by tracking their movements through an arid and rugged area not far from their home. The settlers, of course, had given up all hope of ever finding their children alive."

"And you can give up all hope of finding your pirate lady if you don't shut up!" hissed Terry.

"Was she wearing long boots with a three-inch stacked heel the last time you dipsticks saw her?" asked Tabitha.

We all nodded.

"She's close."

I raised my hand.

"What?" said Terry, angrily.

"How'd you know they were carrying dynamite?"

"Sparkles on the ground back near their vehicle, boofhead. Some of the powder must be leaking."

"Here's the horse head!" said Storm, rubbing a rock that someone, probably Charlotte Badger, had smeared with fresh mud so no one else could read it.

"There's the waterfall!" said Beck.

"And the second waterfall," said Storm, pointing to a cascade of foamy water tumbling off the cliffs, maybe one hundred feet away. Fortunately, the sound of all that rushing water would mask the noise of our final approach, which we'd be doing stealthily, for sure.

"Bully!" said Uncle Richie. "It seems the opals are within our grasp. Thank you, Terry and Tabitha, for your expert guidance."

They both shrugged. "Whatever," said Terry.

"We figured we owed you one for the crocodile save," said Tabitha.

Terry turned to Storm. "You're good with that boomerang."

Storm actually blushed and lovingly tapped the new boomerang tucked under her belt (she'd left the first one in the swamp with the croc). "Thanks."

"Maybe you're half Palawa, too," said Terry with what looked like it might've been a grin. It was hard to tell. His face was still dirty from that mud pie fight.

"Come on, you guys," said Tommy. "We're only like a hundred feet away from snatching the two opals we need to set Mom and Dad free!"

Suddenly, we heard an explosion.

The second waterfall went shooting sideways, opening up like a parted curtain.

When the smoke, dust, and spray cleared, I could see something glistening in the shaft of sunlight cutting through the waterfall.

It was gold.

I figured it might be covered with jewels, too.

Because it had to be one of Bloody Sword Bonito's stolen statues!

WE HOPE THE BLAST DIDN'T BLOW THE OPAL POUCHES OFF CHARLOTTE BADGER'S BELT.

CHAPTER 32

The seven of us went racing up the narrow path along the cliff.

"Coming through," shouted Tommy, elbowing his way through the pack.

"Careful, Tommy," Storm shouted after him. "You might trip on a rock then slip and fall to your death!"

"Or I might nab Charlotte Badger before she escapes from that cave with our two opals!" He kicked his legs into high gear.

"Children?" wheezed Uncle Richie, who was

huffing and puffing and bringing up the rear. "I believe ... a stealthier approach ... might prove ... more advantageous!"

"We can't let her get away!" shouted Beck.

"And I want one of those golden statues!" I hollered.

"Bickford?" cried Uncle Richie, his voice fading behind me. "Keep your eyes on the prize! Stay focused. All we want are those two opals."

"Plus the statues!" I shouted back.

"We're treasure hunters, Uncle Richie!" said Beck. "This is a twofer: A two for one deal we can't pass up!"

Meanwhile, Terry and Tabitha had scurried up the scrubby rocks jutting out from the face of the cliff and were forging their own, much more rugged, path toward the waterfall and cave.

"Children?" shouted a totally winded Uncle Richie, who was leaning on Storm so he wouldn't collapse. "We need to pull together! Remember, teamwork makes the dream work! Alone we do so little, together we can do so much! Talent wins games but teamwork wins championships!"

He might've shouted a few more motivational poster slogans but his voice was soon drowned out by the roar of the waterfall.

"I'll go for one of the statues," I told Beck as spray started pattering our faces. "You go for the opals."

"How come you get the bigger prize?" said Beck.

"Fine. You take the statue. I'll go for the opals."

Beck gave me a look. "Oh. Now you want the opals? Forget it! They're mine."

"Whatever."

We charged through the curtain of cascading water and skidded to a slippery stop on water-soaked stones.

Tommy was already inside the cave, battling off Banjo and Croc in an awesome martial arts duel. We're talking palm-heel strikes, front elbow blows, and forearm blocks. Feet and fists were flying—until Banjo blocked one of Tommy's roundhouse kicks with a solid gold statue. The clunk made Tommy's whole body vibrate and shimmy before he toppled to the ground.

With Tommy out of the picture, Banjo hugged his statue and came running for the mouth of the cave. Croc was right behind him, carrying a bouncing treasure chest dripping with jewels. They were both wearing bulky backpacks.

"Let's hop off, mates!" shouted Charlotte Badger. She was twenty yards deep in the cavern, toting a second jewel-encrusted statue under one arm and charging straight at Beck and me. I could see two pouches swaying on her belt. The opals!

"You go for the statue," I told Beck, "I'll go for the opals!"

"No," said Beck, "we already said that I'd do the opals."

"When did we say that?"

"Ten seconds ago!"

"Change of plans!"

"Too late."

Yes, Beck and I were standing there, fists planted on our hips, screaming at each other when maybe we should've been paying more attention to Charlotte Badger, Banjo, and Croc.

The three pirates barreled right over us, whacking us sideways with a pair of ka-thunking statue swings.

They had Bloody Sword Bonito's treasure *and* the two stolen opals and were racing straight for the backside of the waterfall—taking everything we wanted with them!

CHAPTER 33

The pirates looked like they were going to leap right through the waterfall.

"We have to stop them!" I shouted.

"We can't," said Beck. "We're sitting on our butts in a puddle."

Just then, I heard the shrillest pair of shrieks that's ever pierced my eardrums.

It was a war cry shouted by Terry and Tabitha, the two Tasmanian devils.

"Giirr ngiyani gayaa mari!!!" they chanted as they came swinging through the waterfall,

clinging on to ropey tree roots. *"Dhayn, mari, gayaabali ngiyani."*

(Later we found out what they were screaming as they swung into battle: "We are proud Aboriginal people; we will make the people, the Aboriginal people, proud!")

Terry stuck out his feet and aimed the toes of his shoes straight at Charlotte Badger's face. She ducked, and didn't see Tabitha swinging low to snatch a pouch off her belt.

When they reached the peak of their swing, the twins let go of their woodsy vines, nailed a very Olympics-style landing on the slippery rocks, spun around, and were all set to go chasing after the trio of pirates.

But it was too late.

Charlotte Badger, Banjo, and Croc had already leaped through the roaring wall of foamy water.

"What's going on, dudes?" asked Tommy, as he came limping over to join us.

"We snagged one of the opal bags," said

Tabitha, holding up the velvet pouch she'd ripped off Charlotte Badger's belt.

"But the blooming pikers got away!" added Terry.

"They jumped!" I said. "Off the cliff!"

Terry and his twin sister grabbed hold of a stalagmite rising up from the floor of the cave and stuck their heads through the waterfall. So Beck and I grabbed hold of another slick column and did the same. I guess it's a twins-imitating-twins thing.

We could see Charlotte Badger and her team making a spectacular exit, cradling their treasures tight to their chests. Those backpacks they were all wearing? Those were for the parasails they'd brought along to guarantee a soft landing to their daring waterfall-leap escape. The three pirates were gently drifting down to an inflatable raft with an outboard motor that was just sitting there, waiting for them in Port Phillip Bay.

Storm and Uncle Richie came stomping through the waterfall.

"You let them get away?" said Uncle Richie, sounding way more upset than usual.

"Whoa," said Tommy. "Ease up a little, Uncle Richie. We didn't exactly *let* them do anything."

"They just did it?" said Storm.

"Chya," said Tommy, rubbing his shoulder. "Plus, they kept bonking us with solid gold statues. Those things are worse than aluminum baseball bats."

"We stole this from the lady with dreadlocks," said Tabitha, proudly holding up the pouch she'd torn off Charlotte Badger's belt.

"We looked inside," said Terry. "It's a very fiery black opal. Probably worth a lot of money, right?"

Uncle Richie nodded. "That it is. But, most important, it will help us secure the release of Thomas and Sue Kidd."

"Those are our parents," I said, just in case the Tasmanian twins hadn't been paying attention.

"We know," said Terry with an eye roll.

"Mothers and fathers are more valuable than gold and jewels," added Tabitha.

"Well said, my young friends," remarked Uncle Richie, kind of giving Tommy, Beck, and me the stink eye. "At least you two remained focused on our primary goal and objective."

"Can we keep this?" asked Tabitha, pulling the translucent stone out of its velvet bag and rolling it around so the sunlight slicing through the waterfall could catch its dazzling opalescence.

"Of course you can," said Uncle Richie. "At least until we retrieve the second opal we need to set your parents free."

"And now that Charlotte Badger has taken off for who knows where," said Storm, "where are we going to find the second opal?"

Uncle Richie sighed. "I have no earthly idea."

CHAPTER 34

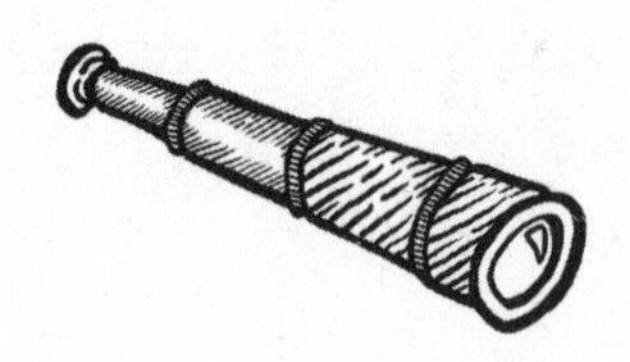

"We're sorry, Uncle Richie," I said after we'd all exited the cave and stood on a precipice, the better to watch the bad guys putter away in their rubber escape raft.

"Bick won't do anything that stupid again," said Beck.

"It wasn't just me!"

"True," said Beck. "But it was mostly you."

"Definitely wasn't me," said Tommy. "I just engaged the villains in a serious exhibition of martial arts skills."

"I had a much better plan," said Storm.

"What was it?" I asked.

"Never mind. It won't work now. Charlotte Badger and the other opal we need are gone."

I slumped my shoulders. "Look, you guys, I'm sorry. I got carried away. It happens whenever I see the glint of jewel-encrusted gold."

"You need to starve your distractions and feed your focus," said Terry.

"You can't track your target if you are easily led astray by shiny objects," added Tabitha.

All of a sudden, the two Tasmanian terrors sounded like the most reasonable members of our expedition. I turned to Uncle Richie.

"I'm sorry. It *was* my fault. What can I do to make it right?"

BICK SAYING HE'S SORRY WHILE TOTALLY LOOKING SORRY.

Uncle Richie clapped his hand firmly on my shoulder and smiled again. "Your best teacher is your last mistake. But, Bick?"

"Yes sir?"

"Next time, let's all work together as a team. It's amazing what you can accomplish if you don't care who gets the credit."

"Right. Thanks."

Storm raised her hand.

"Yes, Storm?" said Uncle Richie.

"As much as I am enjoying this pep talk and seeing Bick squirm, what, exactly, do you suggest we do now?"

Uncle Richie squinted and watched the rubber raft round a bend in the bay and disappear behind a hazy hill on the horizon.

"I'm not sure," said Uncle Richie.

"We should definitely call in that helicopter you and Timbo Tyler set up," said Tommy, his teeth chattering. "They could at least take us someplace where we could change into some dry clothes."

It's true. We were all soaked to the skin.

Jumping in and out of a waterfall will do that to you.

"Maybe Charlotte Badger will go back to her vehicle," said Beck. "The one we found parked on the road. If so, we could track her again."

Tommy shook his head. "That's not gonna happen, Beck. She knows we tailed her. She's probably figured out how we did it, too."

"She's not going to be happy with your Uncle Timbo," Storm told Terry and Tabitha. "If she puts two and two together, she'll realize he was the one who planted the GPS tracker on her vehicle."

"We need to head back to Camp Billabong!" said Terry. "Immediately! We need to protect Uncle Timbo!"

CHAPTER 35

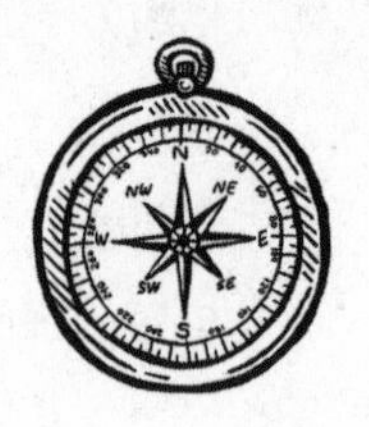

"Right you are," Uncle Richie told the Tasmanian twins. "We'll have the chopper ferry us back. With any luck, we'll beat Ms. Badger and her cronies to the camp. I don't suspect they have a helicopter lined up. They'll, most likely, steal some other vehicle to make their getaway."

"Let's go!" said Tabitha, sounding impatient.

"We need to hurry!" added Terry.

Uncle Richie made the call on his secure satellite phone.

Fifteen minutes later we heard the thumping rotors of a whirlybird, gently descending on a flat patch of weeds that Tabitha and Terry had discovered just to the west of the waterfall. We all

jammed into the back.

Once we were in the air, Uncle Richie called Mr. Tyler and told him to beware. His elbow was in my rib cage the whole call.

"We suspect Charlotte Badger may soon be paying you a visit. And she won't be in a good mood."

On the speakerphone, we heard Mr. Tyler tell Uncle Richie not to worry. "I used to be a bosker, top-shelf spy, working with Thomas and Susan

Kidd and their mates at the CIA, remember? I can handle myself. But thanks for the heads-up, mate. I'll take certain ... precautions."

"Be careful, Uncle Timbo!" shouted Tabitha and Terry.

"No worries, you two. I will."

When Uncle Richie ended that call, Tommy had a brainstorm.

"I need to borrow your phone, Uncle Richie."

"Whom do *you* wish to call?"

"Detective Superintendent Jonathan Michael Ruggiere at the Australian Federal Police. He has the opal Charlotte Badger planted on *The Lost* and now we can bring him the one that was swinging off her belt. That should be proof enough that Mom and Dad aren't crooks. Charlotte Badger is the one Ruggiere should lock up. And, once he does that, he should throw away the key."

"Bully, Thomas! Make the call."

Uncle Richie passed the phone to me, which I handed to Storm, who handed it to Beck, who handed it to Terry, who tossed it to Tommy.

He made the call and made his case. He forgot

to punch the speakerphone button so we only heard one side of the conversation.

"She's connected to two of the stones in the Lightning Ridge Opals case," he said into the phone, shouting to be heard over the din and rattle of the helicopter. "Isn't that proof enough, sir? She's your man. I mean your woman. You know, the person you should toss in jail."

And then Tommy's face went blank as Detective Superintendent Ruggiere said something to him.

"Yes, sir. I understand, sir."

Tommy switched off the phone and handed it back to Uncle Richie.

"So?" I asked. "What'd he tell you?"

"That a deal's a deal. He wants all three opals. Then he reminded me of something."

"What?"

"We only have four and a half more days."

Beck looked at me. I looked at her. I could tell we were both thinking the same thing: We shouldn't've wasted all that time chasing after a glittering gold statue.

The clock was ticking.

PART TWO

INTO THE OUTBACK

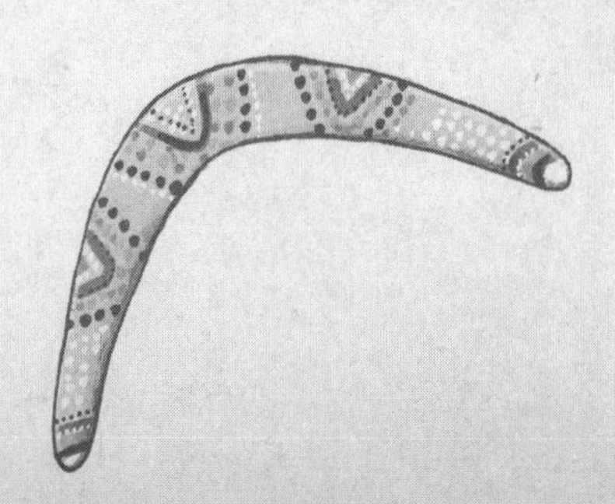

CHAPTER 36

The first thing we noticed when our overstuffed helicopter swooped in for a landing at Camp Billabong?

The airplane we'd rented back in Sydney was no longer on the landing strip where we'd parked it.

"Um, did we take out any insurance when we rented that thing?" Tommy wondered aloud. "I think somebody might've stolen our ride."

"Charlotte Badger!" said Storm, pointing to a bright-yellow Ferrari parked close to the camp's lodge building. Several kangaroos were hanging out, admiring it. "She also stole a 488 GTB. It can go from zero to one hundred kilometers per hour in three point three seconds. She beat us back to Camp Billabong!"

"Strewth," said the chopper pilot. "She was flying faster than we were, and that's no porky."

"Pig?" I said.

Storm shook her head. "Lie. That's no porky means that's no lie."

"Why?" asked Beck.

And all Storm could do was shrug.

Terry and Tabitha nearly ripped the helicopter doors off their hinges the instant the skids touched ground.

"Those pirates could've hurt Uncle Timbo!" shouted Terry.

"They might still be here!" screamed Tabitha. "Their car sure is!"

The two of them barreled out of the whirlybird before the blades had even stopped spinning. They raced across the open yard and tore up the front steps of the building.

"Come on, you guys," said Tommy. "We need to help those two and make sure Timbo Tyler is okay!"

We charged across the open field, sending the herd of 'roos scattering.

When the five of us entered the lodge, we saw Timbo Tyler dusting himself off. His niece and nephew were with him, laughing.

"You really hid up in the ceiling?" asked Terry.

"Too right," said Timbo. He saw us standing breathlessly in the foyer. "Ah, welcome back, Kidd Family Treasure Hunters. I hear you took down

Ms. Badger and nabbed yourselves a precious opal."

"Not us," I said. "It was all Terry and Tabitha. They grabbed the pouch right off the pirate lady's belt. You should've seen them swing into action."

Timbo turned to the twins. "Ripper! You're a pair of fair dinkum heroes. I had no idea you two were the ones who snatched and grabbed the pirate lady's opals."

"Um, didn't they, like, tell you?" asked Tommy.

"Nope. They were too busy making sure I was safe."

"So, how'd you know about the opal?" I asked.

"I heard Charlotte Badger yabbering to her mates about it when they came screaming up to my front door in that Ferrari out there to give me some guff for sending you lot after her. Unfortunately for Ms. Badger, your Uncle Richie had tipped me off so I knew she might be coming."

"Bully!" said Uncle Richie. "Happy to be of assistance, Timbo."

Mr. Tyler gestured toward the grid of foamy pop-up panels over our heads. "Good thing I have a snug and cozy little hiding spot up in the ceiling. When you work in the spy business, you learn to make sure you always have a hidey-hole close by. I was happy as a possum up a gum tree. Even have a small fridge and TV up yonder."

"And you overheard Ms. Badger's conversation with Banjo and Croc?" asked Uncle Richie.

"That I did. Stuck my ear to the floor, which, of course, was their ceiling. Seems they're packing up and heading off for Alice Springs."

"Did they say why?"

"That they did, mate. They're heading into the Outback to search for Lasseter's Gold."

CHAPTER 37

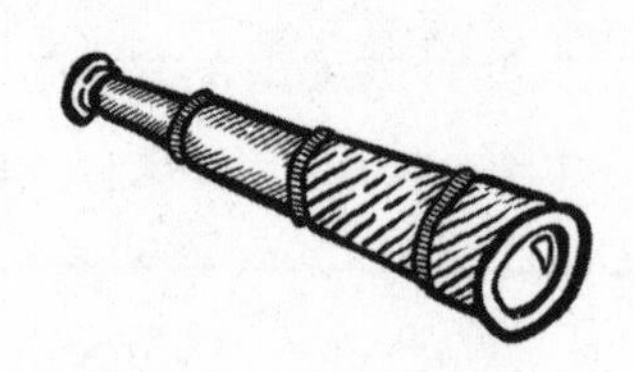

"Lasseter's Gold!" gushed Storm. "A reef of solid gold that Lewis Harold Bell Lasseter claimed to have discovered west of Alice Springs, on the edge of the MacDonnell ranges. But before he could haul out all that gold, the elements turned against him and he got into serious trouble. Wandering through the desert, he had to be rescued by a passing Afghan camel driver who carried him to safety. He went back twice in the next three years, trying to relocate his golden reef, but he couldn't. On the third expedition, he died. A slow and miserable death in the desert."

"He went back to find it several times," Storm continued. "Never could. Neither could anyone else. It remains the greatest lost treasure in all of Australia."

"Too right," said Timbo Tyler. "And Charlotte Badger is dead set on digging it up. Seems the 'sponsor' of her Lasseter expedition made her prove their treasure-hunting bona fides by sending them after Bloody Sword Bonito's loot first. Satisfied that Ms. Badger and her crew know what they're doing, they're moving on to the main event. That's why they stole your airplane, Richie, and several of my navigation charts."

"Who's their sponsor?" asked Uncle Richie.

"They didn't say. But I reckon the bloke is well in and wealthy."

"Do you get to keep the Ferrari?" asked Terry.

That made his Uncle Timbo smile. "No, Terry. It's a stolen vehicle. But, strewth, I reckon I'll have a grand old time driving it back to its rightful owner. Probably be laughing like a kookaburra the whole way!"

"We need to go to Alice Springs, too!" I blurted. "We need to chase after Charlotte Badger and grab that third opal!"

Beck jumped in: "We need it to set Mom and Dad free."

"Bick and Beck are correct," said Uncle Richie. "We need to plot a course for Alice Springs."

“Then you better hurry off to Melbourne,” said Mr. Tyler. “Qantas has a direct flight first thing tomorrow morning.”

“Tomorrow?” I said. “But we need to be there today!”

“Sorry, lad. The evening flights aren’t direct. They’ll make you change planes and wait for hours in far-flung hubs. You’ll end up landing later than you would if you just wait until the morning to take off."

"Very well," said Uncle Richie. "We'll take the first flight tomorrow."

"You'll also be taking Terry and Tabitha, eh?"

"Of course," said Uncle Richie. "Why, I wouldn't think of continuing this adventure without them." He shielded his mouth with a hand so he could whisper to Mr. Tyler. "Tell me: Have the Tasmanian Twins ever flown commercial before?"

"You mean with other people and flight attendants and rules about when you have to fasten your seat belt and when you can and can't go to the toilet?"

"Right."

"Nope. That'll all be new to 'em."

Uncle Richie blinked and smiled and looked like he might be ill.

Timbo Tyler gave him a hearty slap on the back. "Cheer up, mate. Like you said: it should be quite an adventure!"

CHAPTER 38

We spent the night at a hotel near the Melbourne airport.

Uncle Richie called Mom and Dad and gave them an update.

"We're heading off to Alice Springs at the crack of dawn," he told them. "We'll be journeying into the Outback. We suspect that Charlotte Badger has a jump on us. She's already in the desert, hunting for Lasseter's long-lost reef of gold. And she still has that one last opal we need to spring you free from the hoosegow!"

Meanwhile, it turns out that Terry and Tabitha had never stayed in a hotel before. They were fascinated by the ice machine at the end of our hall.

"It just keeps making ice cubes?" Terry asked. "All day, every day?"

"Yep," I told him.

"Why does anybody need that much ice?"

"Well, it's for all the rooms on the floor."

"It's for us, too?"

I nodded.

"And it's free?"

I nodded again.

Ten minutes later, Terry and Tabitha got into an ice chucking battle up and down the hallway. When security came to our floor to tell them to "cease and desist," they returned to our rooms to trampoline on the beds and fling room service trays and food-warming domes like they were boomerangs.

They weren't behaving much better when we boarded the Qantas flight first thing in the morning. They found the bin where the flight attendants stowed the prop oxygen masks for their preflight demonstrations. Terry and Tabitha each put one on and went tearing up and down the aisle screaming, "We are from Mars!" through their noses.

When the flight attendants told them to sit down, they took that as an invitation to kick the seats in front of them.

When other passengers asked them to stop doing that, they figured out how to make pea-shooters with the free peanuts and a paper straw.

Then there was the meal service.

Who knew trays on seat back tables could make such great food catapults or that ham sandwiches could glue themselves to the bottom of the luggage bins?

As we made our final approach into Alice Springs, the flight attendants found some duct tape to make sure the twins were securely fastened to their seats.

Looking out the window, the terrain reminded me of the American Southwest, only redder.

WOOSH!
SQUISH!
HEE-HEE-HEE WEEEEEEE!
?!
KICK!
KICK!
CHIPZ
NEWS
PEANUTS
COLA
CHIPZ
CHOCO
SO MUCH FOR FLYING THE FRIENDLY SKIES.

There was nothing but scrubby ridges, dirt, and a few scattered houses as far as the eye could see. The Outback (what some Australians call Never Never) was, definitely, the middle of nowhere.

We touched down, right on schedule, which was a good thing. We were down to four days before our deal with Detective Superintendent Ruggiere would expire and Mom and Dad would start doing serious time in a former penal colony's penal system.

As we taxied toward the terminal, a fleet of emergency vehicles, their red roof lights swirling, came out to greet us.

Maybe the security folks had heard about the Tasmanian Terrors' behavior in the air.

Maybe we were all going to get arrested, too!

CHAPTER 39

Two air security officers from the Australian Federal Police boarded the plane and had a word with the flight attendants who immediately pointed to Terry and Tabitha.

I could read their lips: "That's them."

The officers nodded. And waited.

When it was our turn to shuffle into the aisle and the seven of us finally made our way to the front of the plane, the two officers blocked our exit.

"Wait 'alf a mo'," said one, holding up his hand.

"You two are up the spout, that's for sure," said the other, eyeballing Terry and Tabitha.

"Huh?" I said.

"They're like the itsy-bitsy spider?" asked Beck.

"'Up the spout' means they're in trouble," whispered Storm.

"Ohhhh," Beck and I said together. "Got it."

"Officers," said Uncle Richie, putting on his best "heh-heh, it was all a joke" voice. "Our young friends here were just a wee bit rambunctious. First time flying Qantas. They were so excited by all the lovely amenities and in-flight service. No harm, no foul."

Terry and Tabitha blew a pair of very wet raspberry lip farts.

The officers looked steamed.

"They're new to commercial airliners," Uncle Richie hurried to explain. "You see, their mother flew them from their remote village in Tasmania to Melbourne in a private prop plane so they could spend time with their uncle."

"You're telling me that these two little brats didn't know how to behave properly?" said the one officer. "Tossing food at folks, kicking seats, fooling around with the air sickness bags?"

His partner muttered what I think had to be a racial slur, maybe something about their Aboriginal ancestry.

Terry and Tabitha both clenched their fists. Uncle Richie placed a calming hand on their shoulders, but his neck hairs were bristling, too. He didn't like the way the officers were looking down their noses at the twins because they had dark skin and wildly curly hair. For the first time since we'd met him, I think Uncle Richie was seriously angry.

"It was all in good fun, I assure you," Uncle Richie explained as calmly as he could for being as mad as he actually was.

A third AFP officer stepped on board the plane. He wore a white shirt with gold leaves on the collar and looked like he might be in charge.

"You the ones chasing after the Lightning Ridge Opals?" he asked Uncle Richie.

"Yes, indeed, we are," said Uncle Richie, brightening and puffing up his chest.

The third officer turned to the other two. "Let them go, Oliver."

"But, chief, these two—"

The man in the white shirt held up his hand before the guy named Oliver could hurl another slur.

"I said let them go. Orders from Sydney. Detective Superintendent Ruggiere himself."

"You're kidding."

"Don't be mooney, Oliver. I never joke around. These orders come straight from the top. Apparently, this scruffy lot is on 'assignment' from Sydney." He turned to Uncle Richie. "Get off this plane. Now."

"Thank you, officer," said Uncle Richie, ushering us all toward the jet bridge. "Detective Superintendent Ruggiere thanks you, too—I'm sure. Tootles!"

"Buh-bye," said the smiling flight attendant.

We all scurried off the plane as quickly as we could.

"Sir?" the officer in charge shouted after Uncle Richie.

"Yes, officer?"

"Good luck chasing those other scoundrels through the Outback. With the young scoundrels you already have on your crew, you're going to need it."

CHAPTER 40

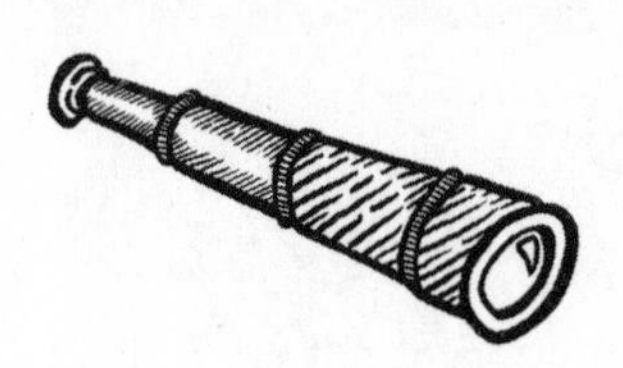

Fortunately, there were all sorts of expedition outfitters in the Alice Springs area.

"It's because we are now in the heart of Australia's Red Center, which, by the way, Australians would spell C-E-N-T-R-E," said Storm, our nonstop tour guide. "There's spectacular scenery everywhere. In fact, we're not too far from the great sandstone rock of Uluru, also known as Ayers Rock. No tour would be complete without watching the mountain-size slab of sandstone change colors at sunset."

SORRY. IT'S KIND OF HARD TO SHOW THE SANDSTONE CHANGING COLORS IN A BLACK-AND-WHITE DRAWING.

"Um, we're kind of in a hurry," I reminded Storm. "We can't afford any detours, no matter how spectacular the sunset. We only have four days left."

"Three and a half," said Beck.

"And," said Tommy, "we're going to need like a day to hustle back to Sydney after we, you know, steal back the final opal if we want to spring Mom and Dad before the deadline expires."

"I don't really want to do any sightseeing," said Storm. "I just memorized too many brochures. It's a bad habit."

"Good," said Tabitha. "We don't like tourists traipsing around Uluru. It is a sacred spot."

"This landscape was created by great ancestral beings," added Terry. "Mom told us all about it. The Anangu people in this area belong to the oldest culture known to man, dating back sixty thousand years."

"So, pfffffft to all the tourists tramping over our sacred rock," said Tabitha, giving us another lip-fart raspberry.

We were crammed into an airport shuttle van hauling us to a place called Afghan Traders where we met Mrs. Walker, whose skin looked like dried leather. I figured she's spent a lot of time in the sun. She was delighted to rent us an awesome Land Rover Defender four by four (the roof popped up to make a tent!) the instant she saw Tabitha and Terry.

"Are you two Palawa?" she asked.

The twins nodded. "On our mother's side," said Terry.

"My mum, too!" said Mrs. Walker with a wheezy laugh. Then she winked. "I like to say I'm half Tasmanian devil!"

"Us, too," said Tabitha.

(Actually, after the incident on the Qantas flight, I might have to go with 100 percent devil for our Tasmanian twins.)

Mrs. Walker was even more pleased to rent us the posh off-road vehicle with an attached trailer filled with water and supplies when Uncle Richie flashed Mom's shiny black credit card.

"Crikey, aren't you the fancy show pony?" she said. "The Defender with the trailer attached is out front. The seven of you should be able to squeeze into her, if you don't mind cramped quarters. I could scrounge up a second vehicle for you in about two hours. Been a bit of a rush on them this week..."

"We're in a bit of a rush, too," said Uncle Richie.

"One Land Rover will be fine," said Tommy.

"We're riding into the Outback," said Storm. "On a quest to find Lasseter's Gold."

"Really?" said Mrs. Walker. "Seems to be a lot of that going around lately. Why, only yesterday, I rented an SUV to a strapping young sheila with a head full of dreadlocks tied back in a bandana. She was traveling with two scruffy looking mates. Said they were off to find Lasseter's Gold, too. I wished them luck. They said they didn't need luck. They had a map."

I gulped a little.

Because the lady with the two mates had to be Charlotte Badger with Banjo and Croc.

And she also had a one-day head start on us!

CHAPTER 41

One thing the tourist books don't tell you?

How boring the Outback can be. Unless you're really into red rocks. Or Mars. It kind of looks like Mars does in one of those NASA rover photos.

Storm, who had memorized all of Mom and Dad's maps and charts for our Australian adventure, acted as our onboard GPS.

"West," she told Tommy, who was behind the wheel.

"Then what?"

"West some more. We need to go up into the MacDonnell Ranges."

Which, of course, were west.

The ride was so boring, even Terry and Tabitha had stopped asking, "Are we there yet?" They knew we weren't. We weren't anywhere except the middle of nowhere. The Never Never.

And Charlotte Badger was probably twenty-four hours ahead of us, deeper into nowheresville.

"Storm?" said Uncle Richie. "Since we still have a great distance to travel, perhaps you could tell us a little more about Mr. Lasseter and his gold. Best to be prepared as we embark upon this grand adventure."

"Um, can't we just listen to the radio?" suggested Tommy, flicking it on.

There was nothing to listen to but static and squelches.

"How about an audiobook?" I suggested. "They sure make the time fly on a long car drive."

"Did you bring one?" asked Beck.

"No."

"We could teach everybody how to blow a didgeridoo," said Tabitha.

"Did you bring one?" Beck asked again.

"No," said Terry. "Sorry."

Then we all sighed. Because we knew there was nothing left to do but listen to Storm's info dump.

"Lasseter had been prospecting for rubies up in the MacDonnell Ranges. He got lost and stumbled across a rich reef of gold. It was a shallow zone of quartz deposits seven miles long, four to seven feet high, and twelve feet wide—all of it speckled with nuggets of gold. He collected a gold specimen and, while trying to return, became hopelessly lost. He was found by an Afghan camel driver. Lasseter was at death's door:

half-starved, dehydrated, and delirious."

Yeah. Sort of like how I feel in the middle of one of Storm's long-winded history lectures.

We were bored out of our brains.

So, with the help of Terry and Tabitha, Beck and I did the only entertaining thing we could think of that didn't require CDs, an iPhone, or a radio. We launched into a four-way Twin Tirade.

"This is hopeless!" I shouted.

"You're hopeless!" shouted Beck.

"You're both hopeless!" said Tabitha.

"So are you, Tabby!" added Terry.

"Tabby sounds like a cat!" I shouted.

"So?" Tabitha shouted back. "Bick sounds like a ballpoint pen!"

Then we really pushed ourselves and launched into some Aussie slang insults we'd picked up on our trip down under.

"You're a dilly!"

"You're a dipstick!"

"You're a drongo!"

"And you're a dork."

We sort of worked our way through the alphabet, taking turns hurling words we didn't really understand (even though Tabitha and Terry sure did).

By the time we got to the *N*s and "ningnong," Tommy had had enough.

He pulled the SUV off the dusty road and into the scrubby bush.

"Snack break!" he shouted. "Everybody out of the vehicle! Now!"

CHAPTER 42

"An excellent suggestion, Thomas," said Uncle Richie as we rumbled off the road (if you could call a rutted strip of dirt a road). "We should all stretch our legs, breathe in some of this fresh Outback air and enjoy some light refreshment."

"We should also tell all the twins to knock it off," mumbled Storm.

"We already have," said Beck.

"Totally," I added.

"Ditto," said Terry and Tabitha.

"Because," I said, "nothing stops a Twin Tirade faster than an official snack break. What have we got in the cargo carrier? Besides water."

"Don't know," Tommy said. "Let's hope Mrs. Walker packed us something tasty."

He opened his door and headed back to the trailer full of supplies. Storm followed him.

"It better not all be Vegemite!" she fumed.

Tommy and Storm freed the bungee cords holding down the tarp tossed over the top of our supplies trailer. The rest of us were right behind them, up on tiptoe, examining the contents.

"Tons of water," said Storm.

"Bully," said Uncle Richie. "One can never have enough *aqua pura* when crossing a desert."

"Check it out," said Tommy. "There's a bunch of military-style Meals Ready to Eat. I think some of them come with M&M's."

"Cool," Beck and I said together.

"Wonder what's in this carton?" said Tommy, cutting open the tape on a cardboard box with the tip of his very long knife. "Huh, it's a bunch of packages of something called Tim Tam chocolate biscuits."

"That's what we call cookies here in Australia," said Terry, grabbing one of the very colorful and shiny wrapped biscuit trays. "Is there milk?"

"Yeah," said Storm. "It's even cold. Mrs. Walker packed it in a cooler."

"Bonzer!" said Tabitha. "We should show this lot how to do the Tim Tam Slam."

"Huh?" I said.

"You bite off the top, bite off the bottom, dunk the biscuit into a glass of milk, and slurp it up through the soft chocolate center like a straw."

"Instant chocolate milk," added Terry.

Okay. Tim Tam Slamming sounded like fun. So, we all gave it a go.

A few cookies later, we were all feeling better. Happier. Chocolate and sugar will do that to you.

After Storm downed half a dozen cookies, she started humming to herself as she drifted off to doodle wavy lines in the ground with the tip of her boomerang. When she'd completed her swirling red-sand masterpiece, Terry and Tabitha froze mid–Tim Tam Slam.

"Why'd you draw that map?" asked Terry.

"It's not a map," said Storm. "It's just the design carved into the sides of one of the didgeridoos I found buried under all the others in that stack back at your uncle's camp. I memorized the markings. Thought they were interesting. Unusual."

"It *is* a map," Terry insisted. "Those are Aboriginal markings and glyphs leading the way to a very specific treasure not far from here."

"Seriously?" said Storm.

Terry and Tabitha both nodded.

"If your drawing is correct," said Tabitha, "it will lead us straight to a very long reef of solid gold!"

Beck and I looked at each other.

"Lasseter's Gold!" we shouted.

CHAPTER 43

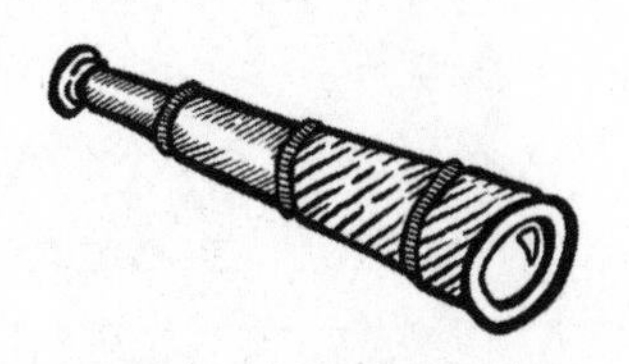

"Wait a second," I said. "Why would anybody carve a treasure map onto a long wooden tube that makes funny noises?"

Terry and Tabitha shook their heads and smiled at me.

"What? You don't think our ancestors, the original people of this land, knew where to find gold?" said Terry.

"Especially once they learned how much gold meant to the white settlers?" added Tabitha.

"Our ancestors were very proficient prospectors, helping settlers find flickering specks of gold in the middle of nowhere," said Terry. "But the

only reward they might receive for their efforts was a new pair of boots—*if* their boss was one of the nicer ones."

"So," said Tabitha, "some of our most clever ancestors started hiding what they knew and translating that knowledge into secret treasure maps carved into stones, boomerangs, or didger-idoos."

"Who says all the gold and jewels of Australia should belong to European settlers?" asked Terry.

"Um, the European settlers?" said Tommy.

"Exactly," said Tabitha. "But, this is our land. Its gold and opals belong to us!"

"But," I said, "we need one of your opals."

"Otherwise," added Beck, "our mother and father might spend the rest of their lives in an Australian jail."

"If I may?" said Uncle Richie. "I suggest we use this newfound 'map' to forge ahead. Remember, we are not really searching for Lasseter's Gold. We have no desire to remove it from the land or to steal it from its true owners, the native people who have lived here for eons. We are only trying to track it down as a means of finding Charlotte Badger and securing the last of the three stolen opals."

"I still have the second one," said Tabitha, patting a buttoned-down pocket on her safari shorts. "Until tonight. Then Terry gets to have it."

"We're taking turns," said Terry.

"Otherwise," said Tabitha, "we'd just be up all

night screaming at each other. 'Give me the opal, give me the opal!'"

"That's the spirit!" boomed Uncle Richie. "Complaining about a problem without proposing a solution is called whining."

"Or whinging," said Storm. "That's what Australians call it."

"Righto," said Terry and Tabitha.

"So, let us proceed," said Uncle Richie. "Storm? Have you memorized the map you scratched into the dirt?"

She nodded.

"Bully! Because we can't really roll up a dirt map, now, can we?"

CHAPTER 44

At sunset, we pitched our tents (they were in that trailer, too), and checked in with Mom and Dad back in Sydney.

Uncle Richie put his satellite phone on speaker mode so we could all listen.

"We completely concur with your plan," said Dad.

"One hundred percent!" added Mom.

"Use your newfound treasure map to pinpoint the location of Lasseter's Gold. Then offer to share that intel with Ms. Badger in exchange for the opal," said Dad.

"While simultaneously sharing your finds with local Aboriginals," said Mom.

They both sounded upbeat, just like they always did. There was no hint in their voices that they were wasting away in a dark and dreary jail cell.

"And Tabitha? Terry?" said Dad.

"Yes, sir?" they both replied.

"Thank you. For this and for everything you have done to keep our family safe."

"No worries."

After the phone call, we whipped up some of the Meals Ready to Eat. Beck and I had minced meat spaghetti. The Tasmanian twins went with the chicken curry. Tommy had beef BBQ, Storm grabbed the Moroccan lamb, and Uncle Richie chowed down on hearty beef stew.

We all gave our concentrated yeast extract packets (Vegemite) to Terry and Tabitha.

"We'll push on at first light," said Uncle Richie, as we all huddled around a small campfire. The sky was full of stars and the moon was shining bright. Only it was upside down.

"Because we're in the Southern Hemisphere," Storm explained. "And Earth is a spherical planet. If you stood on the North Pole and I stood on the South Pole ..."

"We'd both be freezing," said Tommy.

"And our heads would be pointed in the opposite directions. Down would be up, and up would be down."

"Anybody want to slam some more Tim Tams?" I asked, because the night was too awesome to waste on an astronomy lecture.

"Sounds like fun!" said Beck.

"Totally," said Tabitha and Terry, who'd already picked up some American slang.

"We'd best ration our provisions," said Uncle Richie. "We'll set out tomorrow at the crack of dawn."

"When we'll only have three more days left to retrieve the third opal," said Beck.

"But first we have to find Lasseter's gold reef," said Tommy.

"Then we have to find Charlotte Badger," said Beck.

"And we have to find those local Aboriginal tribes, too," said Uncle Richie.

"Phew," I said. "We're going to be busy, busy, busy."

"We also have to battle the Outback," Storm reminded everyone, because she's big on the gruesome and gory stuff. "The sun could kill us if the flies don't do it first. Dust storms can blow up out of nowhere. Then, there are the snakes. And the giant speedy lizards. Not to mention the giant scorpions. And the angry red kangaroos. And the

stampeding herds of wild camels ...

"There are also huge, ginormous feral pigs with curled tusks the size of—"

"Thank you for that, Stephanie," said Uncle Richie, finally cutting her off. "On the bright side, we have plenty of water and enough gasoline to carry us wherever we need to be and then back to Alice Springs. And, most important, we have each other."

I nodded.

Although, at that exact moment, I wasn't sure if having Storm on our side was such a major plus.

CHAPTER 45

We ate a quick breakfast and broke camp.

We had a lot of ground to cover. Dry, treacherous, sun-scorched ground.

"There aren't many roads where we need to go," said Storm, handing Tommy a paper version of the map she'd etched in the sand. "Fortunately, we don't have that far to travel. Only about thirty miles."

"Thirty miles?" said Beck. "That's far, Storm."

"Well, not as far as we've come," I said.

"Right you are, Bick," said Uncle Richie,

clapping me on the back. "And, fortunately for us, our vehicle has something Mr. Lasseter never had: air-conditioning."

Until it didn't.

At approximately mile two as we traversed the rugged terrain, several sharp little red rocks were kicked up from their resting spots by our front tires. Seeking revenge, the rocks leaped up under our hood and cracked our air conditioner's fan.

Tommy stopped the vehicle. Beck and I crawled under the front of the Land Rover to survey the damage.

"It's busted," we reported.

"Can we, like, fix it?" asked Tommy from his perch in the driver's seat.

Our answer was a quick, "Noooooo!"

Because one of those monster-size snakes Storm had told us about the night before was slithering across the dirt, angling to join us in the shady spot under the engine.

We scrambled left, because the extremely poisonous snake was sliding in from the right.

We yanked open the rear door.

"Forget the AC!" shouted Beck.

"Drive!" We shouted that together.

Tommy jammed the pedal to the metal and blasted off. There was no telltale thump beneath our tires. The snake had lived to terrorize another pair of twins dumb enough to crawl around underneath a car in the middle of the Outback.

Storm had also been right about the heat. With no air-conditioning and the sun blazing away mercilessly it was like we were driving across the desert in an E-Z Bake oven—even with the windows down. And with the windows wide open, all sorts of flies the size of gummy bears hitched a ride and tried to drive us bonkers.

We all started doing what Terry and Tabitha called the "Aussie salute." Brushing away flies with our hands.

And then, of course, the engine overheated.

"The coolant's low," said Tommy, repeatedly flicking the dashboard indicator light with his finger, as if that might somehow reset it.

"I saw some spare coolant in the cargo carrier," said Uncle Richie. "You pop the hood, I'll retrieve the coolant jug."

So, Tommy pulled over (again). Steam hissed up along the edges of the SUV's hood. Tommy stepped outside and did a dozen more Aussie salutes. Uncle Richie was flipping at flies with his satellite phone.

He was so busy shooing flies, he didn't see the wild dingo dog stalking him until he heard it start snarling.

"That's a good boy," said Uncle Richie, backing up toward the vehicle. "Don't make any sudden moves, Thomas. Wild dingo attacks on humans are rare, but they are known to happen. They can also be lethal."

"What're you gonna do?" asked Tommy.

"Simple," said Uncle Richie. "Teach this dog to play fetch."

He hurled his satellite phone as far as he could.

The dog went running, chasing after it. He leaped into the air, caught the phone, and came down with it clamped in his jaws.

Then it started trotting away with its trophy.

"No!" shouted Storm. "We need that phone! How else are we going to call Mom and Dad?"

She triumphantly strode out of the Land Rover, unclipped one of the boomerangs attached to her belt, and sent it sailing.

It bonked the dingo in the butt.

The dog yelped.

It also dropped our satellite phone.

And then it took off running over a scrubby knoll.

CHAPTER 46

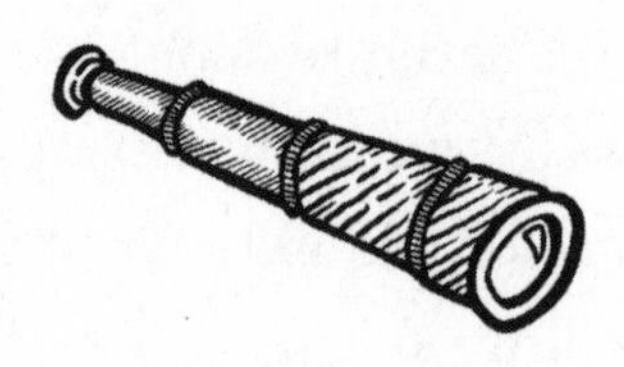

"Woo-hoo!" Beck and I shouted.

"Well done, Storm!" added Terry and Tabitha. "You're a bobby-dazzler boomeranger, for sure."

"Thanks," said Storm, rubbing her shoulder like an ace pitcher who'd just won the World Series. "You guys want to go fetch the phone and my boomerang? I'm sort of winded."

"No worries," said Beck.

She and I climbed out of the SUV. "We'll be right back."

The two of us trotted across the arid red dirt.

After about fifty feet, I scooped up Storm's boomerang.

"There's Uncle Richie's phone," said Beck, scampering off to retrieve it.

As soon as I had the boomerang tucked under my belt, I jogged over to where Beck had found the phone.

"Excellent work," I said.

"We Kidds are like a well-oiled machine," said Beck. "Each one of us doing what we do best."

I nodded. "True, so true. For instance..."

We didn't get a chance to continue our Kidd Family Admiration Society meeting.

Because that dingo Storm had bopped in the butt was back.

And he'd brought friends.

Several of them.

Beck looked at me while I looked at her.

"Run!" we both shouted.

We turned tail and headed back to the hissing SUV.

"Forget adding coolant!" I shouted to Tommy and Uncle Richie. "We need to get out of here. Fast!"

Tommy and Uncle Richie scrambled back into the front seats.

Storm threw open the rear passenger door on her side.

"Here," I said, tossing her back her boomerang. "Do something."

Terry and Tabitha kicked open the rear doors on the other side. Beck and I ducked, so we wouldn't block Storm's shot and scurried around the tail end of the SUV so we could leap through the door Terry and Tabitha had swung open for us.

Storm had already sent her boomerang flying. This time, it swooped through the air like a hovering bird. The dog pack paused, then went chasing after it.

Tommy gunned the whining engine, which really sounded angry—complaining about working so hard without any coolant.

In a flash, we were far away from the dingo pack (which was probably still chasing after Storm's "birdy" boomerang). We were, basically, safe.

"Well done, children," said Uncle Richie and we lurched and bumped our way across the rugged terrain. "Henceforth, we must take extra precautions before leaving the vehicle."

That's when I heard the front axle snap.

"Boulder," said Tommy, gripping the wheel hard. "Didn't see it. Buried under sand."

Then the hood flew open and started spraying steam like a geyser in a national park.

"Hang on, everybody!" cried Uncle Richie. "Brace for impact!"

We did. Just before the front end of our trashed Land Rover nosedived into a sand dune.

Which was hiding more rocks.

The vehicle's front end crunched and buckled. We stuttered to a stop. Tommy flicked off every switch he could. We didn't want fuel mingling with the sparks under the hood.

"Bully," said Uncle Richie, not quite as bullishly as he usually does. He adjusted his hat. "Everyone safe? Any injuries? Broken bones?"

"We're good," I mumbled.

"Fine," said Storm.

"Awesome ride, dude," said Terry, patting Tommy on his shoulder.

"Better than Disneyland," added Tabitha.

"Thanks, dudes."

"Rebecca?" said Uncle Richie. "Might I have that phone? Time to call Mrs. Walker back in Alice Springs. I believe we are in need of a replacement vehicle."

CHAPTER 47

Yep. We were basically stranded in the desert.

"But we're only like five miles away from where the map says we'll find Lasseter's Gold," said Storm.

"We should hike it!" I said.

"Bick's right," said Beck, actually agreeing with me. In public. "We've hiked five miles before. It's easy peasy. No big deal."

"Yes, it is," said Storm, "if those five miles are not in the middle of the sweltering desert. That's how Lasseter died out here. Hiking. He couldn't carry all the water he needed so he became delirious. Before long, he didn't even know where he was or which way was north, east, south, or west. He dropped to the ground. Died. The sun baked away his body and then it bleached his bones."

"Well," I said, "when you put it that way …"

"Fear not, children," said Uncle Richie. "Mrs. Walker runs a reputable and highly regarded operation back there in Alice Springs. I'm sure that, once she learns of our plight, she will dispatch a replacement vehicle, posthaste."

"We're only five miles away from all that gold?" asked Terry.

Storm nodded.

"That stinks worse than a bucket of prawns in the sun," said Tabitha.

"Too right," said Tommy.

"Come on, now," boomed Uncle Richie. "Stiff upper lips, everybody. We have food. We have water. Neither a slithering snake nor a deranged dingo has harmed us this day. And we still have three days to complete our mission."

"Two and a half," I said, squinting up at the sun, which, dead overhead, was sizzling us like bacon in a pan. "It's noon."

Uncle Richie ignored me, consulted our rental agreement, and jabbed some buttons on his satellite phone.

"Ah, yes. Mrs. Walker? Richie Luccio here. We rented that Land Rover from you yesterday? Right. We're the *other* ones searching for Lasseter's Gold. We've run into a bit of a sticky wicket out here in the Outback. I wonder if you can spot our location via your vehicle's GPS indicator. Yes. That's us. Smack dab in the middle of nowhere."

I cupped my hands around my mouth and shouted, "But we're only like five miles from all that gold."

Everybody, including Uncle Richie, looked at me and shook their heads.

"Sorry," I said. "My bad."

We went back to eavesdropping on Uncle Richie's phone call.

"Three days?" he sputtered. "But that's

unacceptable. We have to complete our mission in three days or there will be dire consequences."

Uncle Richie stopped talking. Mrs. Walker was clearly jabbering in his ear.

"Very well. We will stay put. Yes, Mrs. Walker. We certainly understand the dangers and hardships associated with trekking across the Outback on foot. We await your speedy delivery of our new vehicle."

Uncle Richie disconnected the call.

"Three days?" said Tommy.

Uncle Richie nodded grimly. "Maybe two if someone returns their car early. She says that's the best she can offer. All of her off-road vehicles have been rented. The other expedition outfitters in Alice Springs are similarly sold out. Apparently, there is a big festival at Ayers Rock this weekend. And there's nothing near our current location except a few Aboriginal communities. None of which feature gas stations, auto mechanics, or rental car agencies."

"It took us a day and a half to get this far,"

mumbled Storm. "We may not be rescued for four or five days."

"We'll never beat that opal delivery deadline," said Beck.

"Detective Superintendent Ruggiere is going to retire and go to Disneyland," I added. "His replacement will probably be a tough guy."

Terry nodded. "A nasty scut."

"A bantam, bathurst burr of a blitherer," said Tabitha.

"Does that mean they'll be, like, mean and stuff?" asked Tommy.

"Too right," said Terry and Tabitha.

Tommy sighed. "So, Mom and Dad will be stuck in that jail forever."

"I'm sorry, children," said Uncle Richie. "However, I must insist that we make camp, right here, and work out a five-day ration plan with our remaining food and water."

So that's what we did.

When the sun set, we ate a very light dinner and forgot about sucking milk through cookies.

I figured Beck and I would launch into a Twin Tirade. But we didn't. We just didn't have the energy.

Especially when Tommy came to our tent around midnight to give us even more bad news.

"You guys?" he said. "Terry and Tabitha are gone. And, it looks like they took the second opal with them."

CHAPTER 48

"I knew we couldn't trust those two Tasmanian terrors!" I shouted.

"Since when?" asked Beck.

"Since Tommy said they stole our opal."

"Actually," said Storm, "they were the ones who retrieved the opal off Charlotte Badger's belt. They have as much claim to it as any of us."

"Nuh-uh," I said. "Do not."

"Way mature, Bickford," said Beck.

She was right. I was just frustrated, angry, and tired of my clothes looking reddish because of the Outback sand. I was starting to look like a walking cinnamon cookie with a bad rash.

"What's all the hub-bub, children?" asked Uncle Richie, coming over to join us. He was dressed in pajamas, a robe, and a floppy nightcap. What can I say? The guy is stylish, even when he's asleep.

"Terry and Tabitha took off with our opal!" I blurted.

"Actually ..." Storm started.

"Fine! They took off with *the* opal."

"We should go after them!" said Beck. "We could follow their tracks."

"Chya!" said Tommy. "Just like we followed Charlotte Badger's tracks down at Port Phillip Bay!"

Storm raised a finger to make a point. "Um, when we were on the cliffs near Port Phillip Bay, Terry and Tabitha were the ones who did the tracking for us."

"Oh," said Tommy. "Right. Forgot that part."

"It doesn't matter," I said. "We should split up! Tommy and Uncle Richie can go after the Tasmanian Twins and our opal."

"Totally," said Tommy, turning to Uncle Richie. "You might want to change first. Pajamas and a bathrobe are super comfy but they're not the best search and rescue gear. Plus, it could get hotter. The sun might come up."

Uncle Richie nodded. "As it seems to do every day, Thomas."

"Chya."

"While you guys are hunting down our jewel thieves," I said, "Beck, Storm, and I will hike the final five miles over to that buried quartz reef and dig up Lasseter's Gold so we can bargain for the *third* opal! We should leave now. Like Tommy said, we need to do this before the sun comes up."

"Definitely," said Beck. "We have to hike by night. Tomorrow, the temperature could hit forty degrees!"

"Really?" I said. "That's all? That sounds kind of chilly..."

"I'm doing Celsius, Bick, because that's how they measure temperatures in Australia."

"Oh. Right. So what's forty degrees translate into in American temperatures?"

"You mean Fahrenheit? How about one hundred and four?"

I nodded. "So, it's like the desert has a fever ..."

"Exactly."

"Nobody's going anywhere!" said Storm, stomping the ground with her booted feet. Even though it was dark, I could see the angry thunderheads forming behind her eyes. Yep. That's why Mom and Dad gave her the nickname Storm. She doesn't get angry often, but when she does? It's usually a category five rage alert. "Not tonight, not tomorrow, not the day or night after tomorrow! If you do, you'll die."

“Not necessarily,” I protested—as quietly as I could.

“Oh yes you will, Bickford,” replied Storm. “Heat exhaustion. Dehydration. Poisonous snakes. Poisonous spiders. The Australian Outback sun will hit your skin and it will get hot. The tissue under your skin will also get hot. Super hot. Then your bones will start sizzling. You leave this camp, you die!”

CHAPTER 49

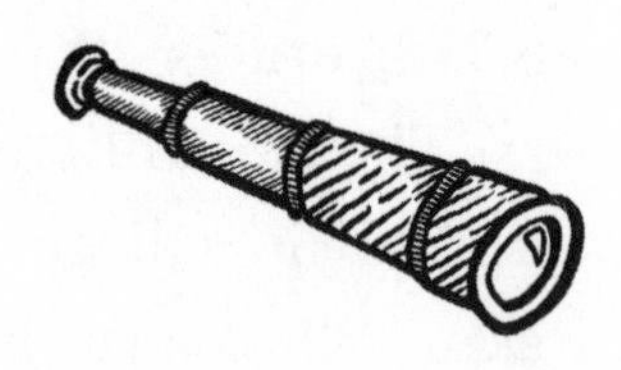

We listened to Storm.

We didn't venture out into the Outback. We stayed right where we were.

Which, by the way, also almost got us killed.

Because the next morning, a swarm of black-and-white birds with beady red eyes started dive-bombing our camp and pecking at us with their pointy beaks. I think they wanted to turn *our* eyeballs red, too.

"They're swooping magpies!" shouted Storm. "It's the biggest wildlife problem in Australia. They think we might harm their newborn chicks! So, they swoop down and attack us before we do!"

"Cover your heads!" shouted Uncle Richie, tossing out pots, pans, and buckets. "The worst thing you can do is fight back!"

"True," said Storm, her tinny voice reverberating underneath the aluminum water bucket she wore for a helmet. "Throwing rocks or sticks at a swooping magpie will only make it want to swoop more. It'll think you really are a threat to its babies!"

"Are magpies the four and twenty blackbirds that got baked into a pie?" Tommy wondered aloud. He was wearing a motorcycle helmet because he always knows how to look cool, even during a magpie swoop.

"No," replied Storm. "But magpies are a protected native species here in Australia, so harming them can lead to penalties and fines."

Great. They could peck out our eyeballs but if we fought back, we'd get a magpie ticket.

After about thirty minutes, the aerial assault ended. The birds flew off to swoop somebody else. We pulled off our improvised helmets. Tommy smoothed out his hair.

"Awesome," he said, checking his reflection in the rearview mirror of our broken-down SUV. "It still has a swoop of its own."

"That settles it," Uncle Richie announced. "No one is going anywhere until our new vehicles arrive. It's far too risky. We are stranded here in what Australians call the woop woop: the middle of nowhere. We have to hope that the other twins, being children of this strange and rugged land, know what they're doing and will, somehow, survive their journey into the scorching desert."

"I'll start researching Aboriginal funeral traditions in case they don't," said Storm. "We might want to do a ceremony like we did for Dad when we thought he was dead." She headed off to her tent and laptop to look into Aboriginal death rituals because, yeah, she's dark like that.

"This is all our fault," I said to Beck.

"I know," she said back. "We never should've broken off from the group when we were doing that dive off the coast of Tonga."

"You're right!" I told her. "That gave Charlotte Badger all the time she needed to plant the purloined opal down in The Room."

"Yep," said Beck. "You let her waltz right in and frame Mom and Dad."

"What? You did it, too! You broke away from the group, too!"

"Only because you did it first."

Yes, what had started as some kind of mutual

misery society had quickly morphed into Twin Tirade 2,016 (or 2,017 if you count that double one we did with the Tasmanian twins; guess we'll have to give it an asterisk in the record books).

"I don't think I did anything first," I told Beck.

"Of course not," she snapped back. "You're a follower, not a leader."

"Hey, I led us back to the shiny stuff on that Tongan dive."

"True. And I was dumb enough to follow you."

"So you're the follower!"

"And you're the guy who forgot to brush his teeth this morning!"

"I'm conserving water!"

"Oh. Deodorant, too?"

"Deodorant has water in it!"

"You can't lick a deodorant stick, Bick!"

"I know," I said, sputtering mad. "So how about, from now on, we try to just work together?"

"Sounds good to me!" screamed Beck.

"Good! No more leading!"

"And no more following!"

"From now on," I hollered, my face turning

purple, “we just have peace and harmony!”

“And togetherness!” Beck hollered back.

“We’re on the same team!” I exploded.

“I know!!!”

“Then why are you two beefing it out like a pair of braying kookaburras?” shouted Terry.

That, of course, brought Twin Tirade 2,017* to a screeching halt.

The Tasmanian Twins were back.

And they’d brought camels.

CHAPTER 50

Terry pointed to the east, where the sun was rising like a furious ball of orange fire.

"We found a stone engraved with a carving over that way," he said.

"It told us that there was a community of our Aboriginal cousins close by," added Tabitha.

"We followed the signs," said Terry.

"And found our people," said Tabitha, pointing to the burly man in a leather cowboy hat riding the lead camel in a string of eight.

"I'm Koa," the man said with a big smile. "My

people are the Arrernte. We're the original people of the Outback. We've been here for tens of thousands of years. Why, we've been here so long, I remember when that sand down there used to be a rock." He tossed back his head and laughed. "Hey, that town you call Alice Springs? It used to be called Mparntwe. Then this lady named Alice moved to town and opened a mattress factory. I kid. I'm a kidder."

"In addition to being extremely funny," said Terry (with an eye roll that Koa couldn't see), "our cousin Koa, here, is an expert camel tour guide."

"It's true," said Koa. "I get nothing but five-star reviews on Yelp *and* TripAdvisor."

"So, it's time for us to ride the final five miles over the desert on camelback!" shouted Tabitha. Then she warbled up a triumphant war cry that sent shivers down my spine. If there were any swooping magpies left in the area, Tabitha's shriek probably sent them swooping off to New Zealand.

"Dudes!" said Tommy, sounding super excited. "We're gonna go get Lasseter's Gold the same way he did: with camels! We're doing it old school!"

"But," muttered Storm, "hopefully not dying old school like Lasseter did."

"Bully!" cried Uncle Richie. "Well done, Terry and Tabitha. Once again, you have proven to be this expedition's heroic saviors. And welcome to you, Koa. I'm sure we'll find your camel expertise as well as your jocund sense of humor to be a beneficial balm during our arduous journey."

We all sort of stared at him. Sometimes, Uncle

Richie says stuff that only people from around 1901 would understand.

"Very well," he continued, "we must pack plenty of provisions, especially water. Yes, it's only five miles to the quartz reef lined with gold, if, of course, Storm's map proves accurate, which, I have no doubt, it will. But we will need water, my camel-riding compatriots. Lots and lots of water. Unlike our dromedary conveyances, the camels, we don't have humps to store it in."

Storm raised her hand.

"Yes?" said Uncle Richie.

"Camels store fat in their humps, not water. If a camel goes without *food,* its hump will start to shrink. The hump has nothing to do with water."

"I see," said Uncle Richie, with a sad sigh. "Alas, another urban, or in this case, desert, legend debunked. Thank you for that, Storm. Hurry up, everybody. We need to pack those provisions and load up the water! Grab the shovels and pick axes, too! Today's the day we go for the gold!"

CHAPTER 51

As we bobbed on camelback across the scorched Mars landscape that is the Red Centre of Australia, I realized we only had a day and a half to retrieve the third opal, fly it back to Sydney, and present it to Detective Superintendent Jonathan Michael Ruggiere.

Otherwise, he'd be off to Disneyland and Mom and Dad would be off to some kind of Australian maximum-security prison.

"By the way," Koa announced over his shoulder from his position at the head of our camel line, "the pirate woman you seek is digging for treasure close to where you seem to be headed."

"You've seen Charlotte Badger?" said Tommy,

who was on the camel right behind Koa's.

"Yes. A tall and imposing woman with many knots tied into her locks of hair."

"Yep. That's her. Did she have two guys with her?"

Koa nodded. "She sure did. They were digging furiously in the sand, not finding much. Say, do you know how to confuse a gold miner?"

"No. How?"

"Show him a row of shovels and tell him to take his pick!"

Koa boomed up another laugh. Tommy scratched his head. I swatted flies.

Meanwhile, Storm gave her camel a slight kick and trotted up to the head of the line to confer with Koa.

"Here is our treasure map," she said, showing Koa what she had transcribed onto a roll of leather, because treasure maps always look way more awesome on some kind of scroll than they do on copier paper.

"X marks the spot, eh?" said Koa, studying the marking.

"Yes," said Storm. "Is Charlotte Badger there?" She tapped the X. "Will she uncover Lasseter's Gold before us?"

Koa shook his head. "No. She is maybe three kilometers north of where we are headed."

"That is splendid news!" cried Uncle Richie. "Once we positively identify the location of Lasseter's gold reef, we will sally forth and parley with Ms. Badger."

"There's going to be a par-tay?" said Tommy.

"No, Thomas. A *parley*. We shall hold a conference with our opposition to discuss terms. We will make a deal with Ms. Badger: our gold for her opal."

"I wish we didn't have to give the gold to those pirates," I whispered to Beck.

"Me, too," she whispered back.

"Me, three," whispered Terry.

Tabitha nodded. "Me, four."

But none of us protested Uncle Richie's plan. We just kept bouncing up and down as our long-legged rides strode across the red-hot desert.

As we slowly humped our way across the

desolate Outback, Uncle Richie used the satellite phone to inform Mom and Dad about our "bully" plan.

"We're nearly to the gold!" he told them. "Once we pinpoint the location and have proof of treasure, we will organize a 'business meeting' with Charlotte Badger. We should have the third opal in our possession before sunset!"

"Wonderful news," I heard Dad reply. "How are Terry and Tabitha?"

"Fine," said Uncle Richie. "In fact, time and again, they have proven to be the most valuable members of this expedition."

"Wonderful."

"Uncle Richie?" It was Mom.

"Yes, Sue?"

"Please hurry. Detective Superintendent Ruggiere dropped by yesterday. He had brochures for Disneyland *and* Knott's Berry Farm. You only have two more days or he and his wife will be gone and Thomas and I will be locked up for at least ten years."

CHAPTER 52

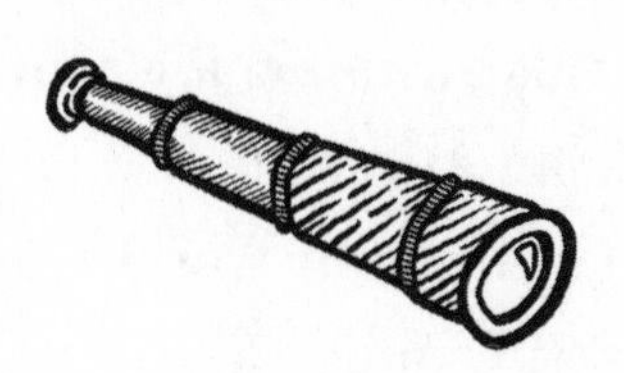

"This is it!" shouted Storm after we crested a hill and came into a long, narrow valley. "We need to start digging!"

"Um, Storm?" said Tommy.

"Yes?"

"This just looks like another strip of sand."

"Because the treasure is buried, Tommy! That's why they call it 'buried treasure'!"

"Oh. Okay. Cool."

Our camels took a knee and we all slid out of our saddles.

We grabbed shovels and picks and started digging. Except Koa. He guzzled water and, while we dug, regaled us with the origins of the Australian slang word "digger."

"The term 'digger' is generally accepted as slang for an Australian soldier, and the myth is that it came from Australians digging trenches at the Battle of Gallipoli in World War One ..."

Fortunately, Tommy, who was digging like a steam shovel, banged his blade into something solid before Koa could bore us with more of his history of slang.

"I've got something!" he shouted.

We all (except Koa, who'd just found our stash of biscuits/cookies in a saddlebag) raced over to help Tommy uncover whatever it was he'd just hit.

"It's quartz," said Terry.

"With gold embedded in it!" added Tabitha.

We brushed away all sorts of sand and exposed a long mound of gold-flecked quartz. Tommy took a pickaxe and gave the glistening vein a good solid whack. A chunk tumbled out.

Storm hoisted it up off the ground, felt its weight, did some quick calculations and gave us her estimate.

"This one piece of quartz?" she said. "There has to be at least a half a million dollars' worth of gold inside it. And there's a ton more where that came from. This whole valley? Under all the sand lies Lasseter's reef of gold worth millions and millions of dollars."

Uncle Richie scooped up a fistful of sparkling rubble.

"Rebecca?" he said. "As I recall, you are the family's number one negotiator."

"Chya," said Tommy. "Beck's the best. When we were on *The Lost,* without Mom or Dad, she worked out all sorts of sweet deals."

"She could talk a hungry dog off a meat truck," I said.

Beck dusted herself off a little. "It's true. I'm good. You want me to negotiate with Charlotte Badger?"

Uncle Richie nodded. "Indeed so."

"No problem. Who's coming with me?"

"Me, of course. And, perhaps Bickford and Thomas?"

"I can soften her up a little for you, Beck," said Tommy. "Show her my gun show." He proceeded to pump both his biceps while saying, "Ka-pow, ka-pow."

Terry and Tabitha did the same thing. "Ka-pow! Ka-pow!"

I would've joined in but, you know. I don't do a lot of bicep curls. Just cheese curls.

"Before we set off to find Ms. Badger," said

Uncle Richie, "we should quickly rebury this quartz vein. After all, what we are offering in exchange for the opal is information about its location."

"Good point," said Storm. She started kicking sand on top of the glittering bank of stone.

We all grabbed our shovels and joined in.

Tommy, who was working harder and faster than anybody (probably to pump up his muscles even more before the visit with Charlotte Badger), took a quick break to lean against his shovel and swipe away some of the sweat dripping down his brow.

"Hey, you guys?" he said.

We all stopped shoveling.

Tommy was gazing up to the crest of a hill on the far side of the valley.

"I just saw a glint of glass up on that bluff," said Tommy. "Like off a pair of binoculars or a spyglass. Somebody's up there watching us."

CHAPTER 53

"No worries, mate," said Koa, squinting up at the ridge. "Those are my associates."

He pulled a slim silver mirror out of his pocket and flashed some kind of signal up to whoever was spying on us from the horizon. The spies flashed back.

"It's some fair dinkum friends from my village," Koa continued. "The ones who have been keeping an eye on your pirate lady, Ms. Badger. They're telling me that she is now only one kilometer away, just on the opposite side of that ridge."

"Frightfully convenient!" said Uncle Richie, smiling broadly. "We shan't have far to travel for our parley."

"When you parley, does that mean you guys are gonna talk French?" asked Tommy.

This time, Uncle Richie just nodded. "Indeed, we might, Tommy. After all, it is the international language of diplomacy."

"Uncle Richie?" said Terry. "Might we borrow your satellite phone to call Tasmania?"

"We'd like to alert our family that we should be home shortly," added Tabitha.

"Mum and Dad like to hide all the breakable objects in cabinets when we're there," said Terry.

"They also lock up all the soda with caffeine," added Tabitha. "The sugary snacks, too."

Uncle Richie nodded. "Wise precautions, I suppose, for any home with active and imaginative young children." He handed them his phone. "Kindly give your parents my fondest regards. And please tell them how valuable you two have been on this treasure quest."

"Will do."

The two twins scurried off so they could talk to their mother and father in private.

"Do you know Morse code?" asked Koa.

"Of course," said Storm.

"Bonzer! I will camel-trot up that crest and join my friends. When you are ready to set off for your meeting with Ms. Badger, signal me. I will signal back her final coordinates."

"Sounds like a plan," said Tommy. "Thanks, man. And thanks for all the jokes. They made the five-mile camel ride just fly by."

Beck and I looked at each other.

Sometimes our big brother is way nicer than he should be.

Koa waved, tapped his camel with a flick of his wispy whip, and scurried off to join his fellow Arrerntes up on the ridge.

I went over to Uncle Richie. I had to try one last time. "Um, is there any way we can keep the gold *and* get the opals? Maybe pull some kind of switcheroo on Charlotte Badger? After all, we're treasure hunters, not treasure-give-away-ers."

He shook his head. "We won't do that, Bickford. Always remember: 'Honesty first; then courage; then brains—and all are indispensable.'"

"Did, uh, Teddy Roosevelt tell you that?"

"Not directly. Besides, don't your parents often donate much of the treasure the Kidd family locates to museums and deserving locals?"

"Yeah," I said. "They do. It's kind of their thing."

"Well, then—I suggest we make it our 'thing' too, eh?"

Beck came over to join us.

"You guys? I'm pumped. This is so going to work. We'll show Charlotte Badger our sample of Lasseter's Gold and, *BAM!* She's going to give us that opal faster than you can say 'Betty Botter bought a bit of butter.'"

"We ready to rock?" said Tommy, holding the leather leads for four camels.

"Totally," said Beck. "Stack them high, watch them fly. On the floor, out the door ..."

"Huh?"

"Just a few motivational quotes that we salespeople employ, Tommy. ABC, bro. Always be closing. Because every no gets me closer to yes ..."

I could tell: Beck was psyching herself up for her "parley" with Charlotte Badger. Getting into sales maven mode.

I HOPE THIS IS ANOTHER ONE OF KOA'S CORNY JOKES.

“Let’s go see Charlotte Badger!” I said, because I knew my twin sib was ready to make her pitch and close the deal.

“Bully!” cried Uncle Richie.

“Okay, you guys,” said Tommy, shielding his eyes with his hand. “Looks like Koa’s up on the ridge. He’s signaling us with his mirror. No, wait. That’s the reflection off a chrome fender. On a motorcycle. Looks like Koa is coming back. On a Harley. And he’s bringing like a dozen motorcycle friends. Huh. One of them has bouncy dreadlocks sticking out of her helmet.”

Yep. Koa was coming back with Charlotte Badger, Croc, Banjo, and about nine other pretty skeevy-looking dudes and dudettes, all of them on roaring motorcycles.

CHAPTER 54

"Those guys weren't keeping an eye on Charlotte Badger!" I shouted over the whine and grind of the gear-shifting motorcycles. "They were keeping an eye on *us*! *For* Charlotte Badger."

Terry and Tabitha came running over to join us. Storm, too.

"Koa has betrayed us!" shouted Terry.

"He also made us listen to all those bad camel jokes," added Tabitha.

"The man is pure evil," said Storm.

Terry tossed the satellite phone back to Uncle Richie. "Sorry about this, you guys," he said.

"We didn't know Koa was a spy!" said Tabitha.

"Honest. We thought he was just one of our cousins with camels."

"And," added Terry, "the corniest comedian in the Outback."

We formed a tight clump as the marauding motorcyclists started circling us. The rumble of their engines scared our cluster of camels. The animals brayed awful, lip-wiggling honks and sprayed the air with camel spittle.

After churning up a whirlwind of sand, Charlotte Badger raised her right arm and the dozen motorcyclists skidded to a stop.

We were surrounded.

"How dare you, cousin Koa!" shouted Terry and Tabitha.

"This is why I wear two watches, boys and girls," said Koa with a booming laugh. "I'm a two-timer."

"You're also not very funny," said Storm, who can be blunt, especially when she's mad, which we all were.

Beck swaggered forward. She was still in killer shark sales mode.

"Nice entrance," she said to Charlotte Badger, who'd just peeled off her helmet and shaken out her dreadlocks. "Impressive. But I can show you something even more impressive. I'm talking about a rich gold deposit first discovered by Lewis Harold Bell Lasseter in 1929. A whole reef of gold, stretching for maybe a mile, or you know ..."

"One point six zero nine three four kilometers," said Storm.

Beck snapped her fingers. "Exactly. I'm talking about the long-lost and legendary treasure known throughout Australia as Lasseter's Gold. Why, it's the biggest plunder in the land down under. And it's all yours, Charlotte Badger, today only, for the low, low price of just one opal."

Beck gestured toward the velvet pouch tied to Badger's wide swashbuckler belt.

"So, do we have a deal?" said Beck. "This is a limited time only offer. Void where prohibited. Actual size of gold reef may vary."

Charlotte Badger started clapping. Sarcastically.

I don't think she was buying what Beck was selling!

CHAPTER 55

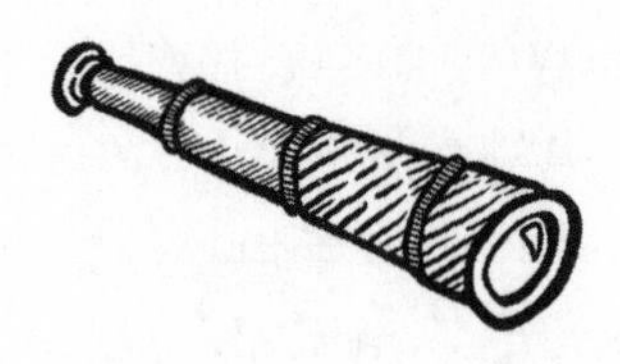

"Nice sales pitch, kid," Charlotte Badger said to Beck. "You should be on TV. Speaking of opals ..." She glared at Terry and Tabitha. "Where's the one you two little Tasmanian devils stole from me on the cliffs?"

"We, uh, lost it," said Terry.

"And, we're not devils," said Tabitha. "We are Aboriginals from Tasmania. Our mother is a proud Palawa!"

"Crikey. All you little nippers are full of useless information, aren't you, now?"

"Don't worry about the opals," said Tommy, sauntering forward, wiggling his eyebrows the

way he does when he's trying to flirt with a pretty girl. "I'll pick up something even shinier for you the next time I'm diving for treasure—at the jewelry store."

"Ha," laughed Croc. "Listen to this one."

"A right little Romeo," chuckled Banjo.

"I don't need your shiny baubles, little boy," Charlotte hissed at Tommy.

"Um, I'm actually a teenager, not a boy ..."

Charlotte Badger ignored Tommy, swiveled in her motorcycle seat, and turned on Beck.

"And I don't need *you* to show me where Lasseter's Gold is buried. Why? Because you already did, lassie, when you blithering duffers dug it up for all to see! I snapped a few photos with my camera. It has a very good, very long telephoto lens on it."

That's what Tommy had seen glinting up on the ridge, I realized. A camera lens.

"And *I* saw where the gold reef is buried, too," said Koa. "Remember? I was here when you guys dug it up. It's right there, underneath all that sand!"

He pointed at the dirt to his right.

"Or, it could've been under that sand. The stuff over there."

"You can have the gold!" said Beck. "All of it. Just give us that opal. We need it to free our parents."

"Aw, isn't that sweet," teased Banjo.

"The wittle girl wants to save her mommy and daddy," added Croc.

Charlotte Badger tossed back her head and laughed. I think she eats a lot of sweets. Her teeth, the ones she had left, were stained brown.

"Sorry," said Charlotte Badger. "That's not gonna happen, peach. My sponsor wants all the gold and *both* the opals, too." Now she was eyeballing Terry and Tabitha. "He thinks it'll make a nice story for the telly. Australia's long-lost treasures found. Two of the Lightning Ridge Opals. All of Lasseter's Gold."

"And what, pray tell, is your sponsor giving you in return for all this treasure?" asked Uncle Richie.

"My own TV show," said Charlotte Badger. "Plus half of the loot."

"Charlotte's gonna be the 'Wonder from Down Under,'" said Croc. "We're gonna be her sidekicks. On TV!"

"The ladies love the sidekicks," added Banjo.

"All right, boys," Charlotte ordered, climbing off her motorcycle. "You go with Koa and start digging. Over there. We need to uncover the whole reef." Koa and five other bikers dismounted and grabbed tools from our pile. "The rest of you lot? You're going to help me persuade our two little curly-haired friends here to cough up that opal they stole off my belt!"

Six very scary, very hairy thugs climbed off their rides and started punching their palms with their fists.

Then, following Charlotte Badger, they started to slowly stroll over to Terry and Tabitha.

CHAPTER 56

"We need to do something!" I whispered urgently.

"Actually," Storm whispered back, even more urgently, "we need to do a series of somethings in a synchronized sequence. Tommy, Bick, Beck, Terry, and Tabitha? Hop on a motorcycle, kick up a dust storm. Uncle Richie?"

"Yes?"

"You and I will go wrangle the camels!"

She gestured to where the eight dromedaries were, unbelievably, calmly hanging out in a clump.

"Capital idea."

So, while Charlotte Badger and her heavies slowly made their way across the sand with their long coats flapping in the arid breeze (probably because they thought the slow-mo moves made them look super intimidating and cool), Beck, Tommy, Terry, Tabitha, and I dashed off to grab one of the six empty motorbikes the digging crew had left behind.

We were all pretty speedy, too. Especially the Tasmanian twins, who let loose with another war cry as they hopped on the nearest motorcycle and kick-started the gnarly choppers to roaring life. Beck and I are awesome on motorbikes, too. Tommy? He's probably the most awesome of us all. In no time, the five of us were cutting donuts and kicking up angry clouds of red dust that spewed all over Charlotte Badger and her six sand-sucking minions.

Meanwhile, Uncle Richie and Storm riled up our camel herd and sent them stampeding toward Koa and the bad guys working with picks and shovels, trying to dig up the golden reef.

Koa tried to call off the camel charge with a

series of whistles and mouth clicks, but the camels were done paying attention to him. Maybe they knew he was a traitor, too. Anyway, the screeching, honking, spitting, hoof-stomping camels scared Koa and the others right out of their narrow ditch.

While both groups were distracted, Storm slipped her trusty boomerang off of her belt.

"Let 'er rip!" shouted Terry, as his motorcycle

fishtailed up another shaft of sand into Charlotte Badger's eyes.

Storm squinted. Took careful aim. Somehow, she located her target in the center of that cyclone cloud of swirling sand and sent her boomerang twirling through the air. The front tip clipped the pouch off Charlotte Badger's belt. The rear tip snagged its leather strap, which wrapped itself around the boomerang in a tightening loop. Wobbling slightly, the flying wooden wedge brought the opal bag back to Storm and Uncle Richie. It was a genius toss. If Storm had thrown her boomerang in some kind of Olympic competition, she would've received tens or, even, elevens from all the judges.

"We have what we came for!" shouted Uncle Richie after Storm unwrapped the pouch from her weapon. "It is time to evacuate this area!"

"Stop them!" screamed Charlotte. "They're nothin' but a bunch of jewel thieves."

Uncle Richie and Storm took off running.

But, to be honest, neither one is very fast. The six guys in the ditch, who didn't have to worry about our hissing camels any more (they'd kept running for the hills) started chasing after them.

So, the five of us on motorcycles spun out of our circular pattern to go help Storm and Uncle Richie.

But that meant Charlotte Badger and the other goons weren't being sprayed by sand anymore. They were free to charge after Storm and Uncle Richie, too.

Both of them were chugging as best they could across the desert, but running in sand is sort of like running in the shallow end of a swimming pool. It slows you down.

And we didn't have enough motorcycles to block all their pursuers.

Two wild-looking guys with shovels were only ten feet behind Storm and Uncle Richie.

Which meant they were only ten feet away from snatching back that opal we so desperately needed!

CHAPTER 57

Suddenly, a shrill war cry screeched up over the horizon.

It was so loud and jarring, it even drowned out the din of our snarling motorcycles. I cut off my engine to try and figure out what was going on.

Those two dudes with the shovels chasing Storm and Uncle Richie?

They were frozen in their tracks because they saw it before I did.

The deafening noise had been warbled up by a hundred or maybe two hundred Aboriginal warriors lining the crest of a sandy knoll in a wild assortment of dune buggies and desert vehicles.

The cavalry (whoever they were) had ridden to our rescue. It was like something out of a Hollywood movie.

I noticed that the scary band of marauders charging down the hill had something the pirates had forgotten to bring to the party: weapons! I mean Charlotte Badger, Banjo, and Croc had a couple of swords and daggers, but these guys in the crazy sand buggies had rifles.

We'd all cut off our motorbikes to marvel at the mob charging down into our dusty valley.

"Who are those guys?" said Beck. "The pirate cavalry?"

"No," said Terry. "They are our cousins. The first people of the Outback. The Arrernte."

"Won't they be on Koa's side?" I asked. "He's gone full-blown pirate on us."

Tabitha shook her head. "No. The leaders of the village warned us about Koa the camel wrangler. Told us to keep our eye on him."

"So," said Terry, "when we figured out what he was up to, we borrowed your Uncle Richie's satellite phone and called our true friends and cousins."

"They got here pretty quickly," said Beck.

"Hey, it's their desert," said Tabitha. "They know how to rumble across it fast."

Now Charlotte Badger and her twelve flunkies were the ones penned in by charging marauders. The Arrernte warriors had them surrounded, with like six circles of vehicles and weapons.

A very noble-looking man stood up in one of the vehicles. "Welcome to the Arrernte Nation," he proclaimed. "This has been our land for more than forty thousand years."

Tommy whistled. He was impressed.

"That's Jabiru," Terry whispered. "He's like their leader. He was the first one to warn us about Koa."

"We are seventy-five hundred strong," the man named Jabiru continued. "You are twelve. You should leave our land."

"Get out of our desert!" shouted Tabitha.

All the Arrernte warriors laughed when she did.

In the distance, I heard the thumping blades of a heavy helicopter.

"No worries, mate," Charlotte Badger said with a sly wink to Jabiru. "We'll be leaving straightaway. Our ride just arrived. Oh, do us a favor: don't touch our gold while we're gone."

Jabiru laughed. "*Your* gold? Ha. I think you are forgetting who has laid claim to this land for *forty thousand years.*"

More laughter from his kin.

The helicopter swooped down like a magpie with whirling blades on its head and tail.

I couldn't believe what was painted on the side of the chopper!

NCTE!

That meant Mom and Dad's number one nemesis was about to make a surprise guest appearance in the Australian Outback!

CHAPTER 58

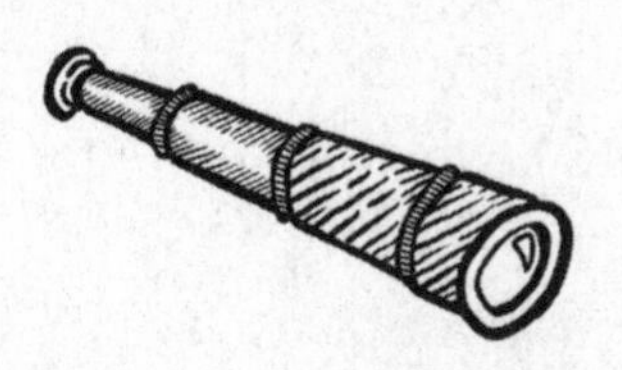

"Collier!" said Tommy, spitting out the "K" sound in the name.

NCTE was short for Nathan Collier's Treasure Expeditions. Collier, who always dresses in an explorer's costume and keeps his greasy hair slicked back tight, except for a spit curl dangling over his forehead, is our parents' number one rival.

He's also a terrible treasure hunter. He couldn't even find the toy surprise buried inside a box of cereal. Instead, he follows Mom and Dad or us Kidd kids around, lets us find the treasure, then he drops in and tries to claim our treasure as his own. He then puts his "extraordinary explorations and exploits" on TV. He's one of the Treasure Channel's biggest stars—right up there with the dog, Winky, who digs up interesting things in people's backyards (I loved the *Winky!* episode about a buried bag of dirty diapers).

Nathan Collier was hanging out of the door of his large, cargo-size helicopter, with a bullhorn.

"Don't you dare harm a knotted hair on Charlotte Badger's head," he barked through his megaphone, which squealed when he squeezed the Talk button. "With my mentoring, she's going to be the next big star on the Treasure Channel. She's gonna be our Kardashian."

"Give me my opals!" Badger snarled at the Tasmanian Twins. "I need them for TV."

"Ha!" laughed Beck, Terry, Tabitha, and me, simultaneously. It's a twin thing.

"Both of the black opals in our possession were stolen twenty years ago!" proclaimed Uncle

Richie. "They shall now be returned to the proper Australian authorities in Sydney."

"They will also set our parents free!" cried Storm, raising a defiant fist to the sky.

When she did that, the entire army of Arrernte warriors cheered, honked their horns, and rattled their weapons. I have a feeling Storm would've made a great Joan of Arc.

"Very well, Kidd Family Treasure Hunters," Nathan Collier declared through his bullhorn. "You may keep the opals. But Lasseter's Gold belongs to me and Ms. Badger."

"Says who?" shouted Jabiru.

"Me!"

"Really? You and what army?"

This time, Storm (whose photographic memory extends to memorizing pitch perfect snatches of tunes she's heard) warbled up the Arrernte war cry. When she did, more than two hundred voices echoed it in response. I even gave it a try, although I sounded more like a belching emu.

"This gold, good sir," declared Uncle Richie, "has always belonged to the people who have lived on this land long before the dawn of European history on this continent. This is not Lasseter's Gold. It is the Arrernte people's gold as it was in the beginning, is now, and ever more shall be!"

There were more cheers, whoops, and weapon rattling.

Nathan Collier shook a fist at us. "Curses! You Kidd kids have not heard the last of me! You, either, you two little Tasmanian devils! Come on, Charlotte. It's time to make our grand exit. He who fights and runs away lives to fight another day!"

With that, a rope ladder was unfurled from the hovering helicopter. Charlotte Badger and her twelve scurvy pirates scampered up it like they were climbing the rigging on a mizzenmast.

Or rats fleeing a sinking ship.

CHAPTER 59

"Thank you, Jabiru," Uncle Richie said to the Arrerntes' leader. "You saved us from certain danger and, perhaps, even death. And now, if I may be so bold, I would like to request a favor from you."

"Certainly, wise old-timer," said Jabiru. "For even though this vein of gold has, as you said, always belonged to us, none of us could remember where to find it until you and the young Tasmanians came along. What can we do for you, old-timer?"

I was going to suggest, "maybe you could quit calling him old-timer," but Uncle Richie had a more practical request.

"Might we borrow a pair of the swiftest vehicles in your fleet? We need to transport our two opals to Sydney as rapidly as possible. More lives hang in the balance."

"Certainly," said Jabiru. "Why, with Lasseter's Gold, we will be able to purchase an entire fleet of replacement vehicles!"

"Bully!" said Uncle Richie. He turned to us. "Quickly, children. Gather up some water and whatever provisions you might need. We are racing back to Alice Springs. He tossed Tommy the satellite telephone. "Thomas? Kindly procure us another private jet."

"Kewl. Do I get to fly it again?"

Beck, Storm, and I were standing behind Tommy frantically shaking our heads "No." Beck and I were even making prayer gestures, pleading with Uncle Richie.

"We shall see, Thomas," said Uncle Richie. "We shall see."

Hopefully, that was his polite way of saying, "No way, Tailspin Tommy."

The seven of us hopped into two very fast

desert vehicles and raced back to Alice Springs where Tommy had chartered us the fastest jet available at the airport. It was dusk by the time we took off. We were running out of time!

"Bummer," said Tommy when we were all strapped into our seats. "This jet wasn't on my Xbox flight simulator program. I don't know how to fly it."

"Bummer, indeed," said Uncle Richie. "Fortunately, I am certified to fly it and, having had several strong cups of coffee, I am ready to jet us back to Sydney!"

"Hurry!" I said. "The clock is ticking. It's nearly tomorrow."

Yep. We were approaching our final day. Our week was almost over.

As the jet thundered down the runway and lifted off, I closed my eyes and imagined Detective Superintendent Ruggiere filling out his retirement papers and packing Hawaiian shirts for his family's long-delayed vacation to America.

We landed without incident (because Tommy

was nowhere near the controls) in Sydney and found a van that would haul the seven of us down to Long Bay Correctional Complex.

"Just visiting or doing jail time?" the chatty driver asked.

"Just visiting," said Storm, sounding like a square on a Monopoly board.

"Good on you," said the driver.

"Our parents are the ones behind bars," I said.

"But not for long!" added Beck.

"You lot going to bust them out, eh?" said the driver.

"Indeed, we are, good man," said Uncle Richie. Then he thumped the dashboard. "If you don't mind: more haste, less chitchat. We are in something of a hurry."

The driver nodded and accelerated. "Most blokes planning a jailbreak usually are."

"Indeed! For the sun is up. We are nearly out of time!"

We made it to the jail. There was a long line of visitors. It took what seemed like hours for us to be screened by security. When we finally cleared the metal detectors, we went dashing up the corridor to where visitors could meet with prisoners.

We rounded a corner.

And practically bulldozed over Detective Superintendent Ruggiere who was strolling up the hall whistling "It's a Small World (After All)."

He had a very official-looking sheaf of papers in his hand.

ANYONE WITH BUSINESS TO BRING BEFORE ME, SPEAK NOW OR FOREVER HOLD YOUR PEACE. IN THIRTY MINUTES, I'M OUTTA HERE! HANG ON, GOOFY. HERE WE COME!
SCREEECH!!!
SCREEECH!!!

CHAPTER 60

"Ah, Detective Superintendent Ruggiere!" said Uncle Richie.

He looked at his watch. "Only for twenty-nine more minutes."

"Then I shall be brief. We have brought you the second and third Lightning Ridge opals. With them, you now have the complete set and know that Thomas and Susan Kidd were framed on board *The Lost*. Your twenty-year-old cold case can now be closed." Uncle Richie handed the detective the pair of velvet pouches we had ripped off Charlotte Badger's belt. "You and the AFP are now in possession of all three missing gemstones: The Black Prince of the Inland Sea, the Pride of Australis, and the Black Galaxy!"

"Crikey," said Ruggiere. "You lot did it. You pulled off the impossible."

"We also found Lasseter's Gold," I told him, "but we're not here to talk about gold. We're here to talk about setting our mom and dad free."

Ruggiere nodded. "A deal is a deal." He glanced at his watch. "Shirley's waited this long to go to Disney, she can wait another blooming minute or two. Come along, lads and lassies. We need to fill out a few release papers for your parents!"

In no time at all, Mom and Dad were walking out of the prison in their own clothes instead of the orange jumpsuits they'd been wearing all week. They were free. We were all back together again. Detective Ruggiere was on his way to the airport and retirement. I told him to be sure to check out Space Mountain.

"Well done, children," said Dad. "Your mother and I are very proud of you. You, too, Richie."

"You guys should really thank Terry and

Tabitha," said Tommy. "They, like, saved our bacon a bazillion times."

Mom grinned. "As we knew they would."

"Huh?" Beck and I said at the same time.

"Why do you think we suggested you go visit our former colleague Timbo Tyler?" Dad said with a soft chuckle.

"He'd informed us that his niece and nephew would be visiting when we arrived in Australia," Mom continued. "He also informed us of their incredible talents and survival skills."

Dad propped a proud hand on both of the Tasmanian Twins' shoulders. "They know this country and they know how to persevere in the harshest of conditions. We knew you five would be safe if they were traveling with you."

"So," said Tommy, "they were like our babysitters?"

Mom and Dad nodded.

"Awesome," said Tommy. "Because, like I said, if it weren't for those two little Tasmanian terrors, the rest of us would be totally dead right now."

Storm nodded and elaborated. "We'd be nothing but five piles of bleached bones scattered in the Outback. Our carcasses picked clean by roving packs of dingo dogs. Our eyes plucked out by swooping magpies." Yeah. She's morbid that way.

"Where's my favorite niece and nephew?" boomed a jolly voice from an Aussie Troopie that'd just pulled into the prison parking lot. It was Timbo Tyler.

He climbed out of the vehicle. Terry and Tabitha ran over to greet him and he caught them both up in a huge hug.

"Strewth, you two are fair dinkum heroes!" said Timbo. "You've earned some Vegemite ice cream, that's for sure."

"How about mint chocolate chip instead?" said Terry.

"With sprinkles," added Tabitha.

"You have a deal."

Mom and Dad went over and bear-hugged Timbo Tyler.

"Your family saved our family," said Dad.

"Aw, they're all good kids. Reckon they saved each other. And you gave all that gold you found to the locals?"

"That we did," said Uncle Richie. "It seemed only fair."

"Good on you. Who knew I had a didgeridoo with a treasure map painted on it?"

We had a nice visit there in the prison parking lot.

But then it came time to say good-bye, which was kind of hard. Especially for me and Beck and Tabitha and Terry.

"We sort of misjudged you guys when we first met," I confessed. "We thought you were a pair of wild Tasmanian devils."

"And we thought you were a pair of American twits," said Terry.

"We were wrong," I told him.

"We were, too."

Then we all shook hands. And hugged.

And launched into a quadruple Twin Tirade—just for fun.

It was a beautiful thing.

WHAT'S UP WITH VEGEMITE? WHY WOULD ANYBODY EAT MASHED YEAST?
HOW COME AMERICANS DON'T DO THE DIDGERIDOO AS MUCH AS THEY OUGHT TO?
THEY REALLY KE VEGEMITE CREAM? IF SO, HY???
YOUR SKY'S UPSIDE DOWN AND YOUR TOILETS SWIRL BACKWARD.
SO? YOU HAVE YOUR SEASONS UPSIDE DOWN. DECEMBER SHOULD BE IN THE SUMMER!

CHAPTER 61

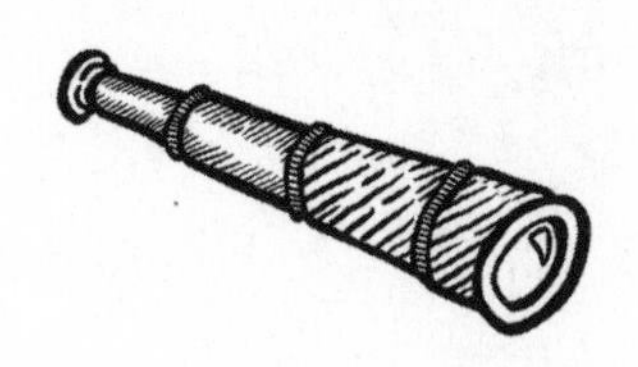

The Tylers headed back to Camp Billabong.

We headed off to Sydney Harbour where *The Lost* was released by the Australian Border Force.

"Thanks for your help in retrieving the Lightning Ridge Opals, mates," said the customs officer who gave us a crisp salute when we reboarded our ship.

"You're welcome," said Tommy. "Thanks for looking out for our vessel."

"Let's get ready to shove off," said Dad.

"Aye, aye!" we all said in reply and, like a well-oiled machine, we all took care of our individual tasks and readied *The Lost* for powering out of the port. Tommy inspected the engine and bilge for leaks. Beck and I checked the fuel and oil levels. Storm powered up the navigational computer. Mom and Dad ran through a series of safety checks. Uncle Richie went down into the galley to make sandwiches.

In no time at all, we were puttering away from Sydney Harbour, taking one last look at the bridge and the Opera House as they faded behind us.

We were ready to set sail for who knows where and who knows what.

"Hey," said Beck, "we should go visit Antarctica. It's the only continent we haven't visited!"

"Because penguins don't bury treasure," I told her.

"It would only take us two days to sail there," reported Storm.

"We could stop off at New Zealand on the way,"

suggested Tommy. "That's where they filmed all the *Lord of the Rings* movies!"

"But what kind of treasure are we going to hunt in Antarctica?" I asked.

"Antarctica is home to some of the oldest ice in the world," said Storm.

"Seriously?" I said. "We're going to go dig up ancient ice? It would melt before we could donate it to a museum."

And while we debated where we might sail

next, Mom and Dad stood up in the wheelhouse, just holding each other tight, staring off at the horizon. There were big smiles on both their faces.

I think they were just happy to be free.

To have their family safe and all together.

And to sail wherever the fair winds and gentle tides might take us.

Hunting for your next THRILLING ADVENTURE?

Join us! Read the whole
TREASURE HUNTERS SERIES.

JAMES PATTERSON received the Literarian Award for Outstanding Service to the American Literary Community from the National Book Foundation. He holds the Guinness World Record for the most #1 *New York Times* bestsellers, including *Max Einstein, Middle School, I Funny,* and *Jacky Ha-Ha,* and his books have sold more than 385 million copies worldwide. A tireless champion of the power of books and reading, Patterson created a children's book imprint, JIMMY Patterson Books, whose mission is simple: "We want every kid who finishes a JIMMY Book to say, 'PLEASE GIVE ME ANOTHER BOOK.'" He has donated more than three million books to students and soldiers and funds more than four hundred Teacher and Writer Education Scholarships at twenty-one colleges and universities. He has also donated millions of dollars to independent bookstores and school libraries. Patterson invests proceeds from the sales of JIMMY Patterson Books in pro-reading initiatives.

CHRIS GRABENSTEIN is a *New York Times* bestselling author who has collaborated with James Patterson on the I Funny, Jacky Ha-Ha, Treasure Hunters, and House of Robots series, as well as *Max Einstein: The Genius Experiment, Word of Mouse, Katt vs. Dogg, Pottymouth and Stoopid, Laugh Out Loud,* and *Daniel X: Armageddon.* He lives in New York City.

JULIANA NEUFELD is an award-winning illustrator who has also worked with James Patterson on the Treasure Hunters and House of Robots series. Her drawings can be found in books, on album covers, and in nooks and crannies throughout the internet. She lives in Toronto.